I0695052

her SLEUTH

SAMANTHA COLE

To my mom, dad, and brother. Thanks for always believing in me.

Acknowledgements

Thanks to Jessica, Julie, and Brandie—you gals are the best!

Thanks to the rest of my beta readers—Charla, Jen, Felisha, and Abby! (And congrats on the little one on the way, Abby!)

As always, thanks to my incredible editor, Eve Arroyo!

Thanks to my awesome PA, Maria Celaschi Clark!

Thanks to my fantastic Sexy Six-Pack Sirens Facebook group! I can never thank you enough for your support, shoutouts, and friendship. You all are amazing!

Thanks to authors Catrina Courtenay, Cristin Harber, and JB Havens for answering questions and letting me bounce ideas off of you.

Thanks to the authors who paved the road for me with their amazing series! Without you leading the way, the Trident Security Series and Malone Brother Series would have never been written—Cherise Sinclair, Lexi Blake, Cristin Harber, Angel Payne, Kennedy Layne, Suzanne Brockmann, Susan Stoker, Jerrie Alexander, Christy Reece, and so many more!

Author's Note

As usual with fiction, several liberties have been taken and facts skewed to fit the story, including people, places, and street names in Dare County, North Carolina, and its surrounding areas. Any discrepancies are either intentional for the story line or because of my own errors.

I have full respect for the members of the United States military and the various members of law enforcement and thank them for their continuing service to making this country as safe and free as possible.

Guide to Law Enforcement Acronyms

- AFIS— Automated Fingerprint Identification System*
- BCI—Bureau of Criminal Investigations
- CODIS—Combined DNA Index System*
- NCIC—National Crime Information Center*
- N-DEx—Law Enforcement National Data Exchange*
- SAC—Special Agent in Charge (FBI)
- SBI—State Bureau of Investigations (North Carolina)
- UNSUB—Unknown subject (suspect)
- VCIN—North Carolina Criminal Information Network

*Run by the Federal Bureau of Investigations (FBI)

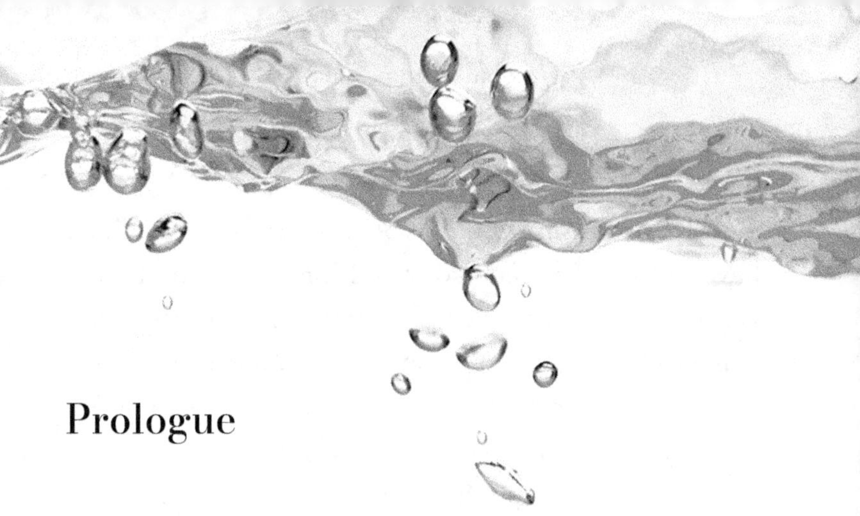

Prologue

The dance floor vibrated with the deafening beat filling the bar. As usual, the nightclub was packed—Saturday night was party night, after all. In tandem with the music, strobe lights pierced the dimly lit room and bounced off the gyrating bodies on the dance floor. The black walls and red accents throughout Visions, the hottest dance club in the area, made it feel more like Sin City. Some of the occupants were just out for a good time, while others were looking for someone to hook up with for either short or long-term companionship. And for at least one person, it was something more. It was the perfect place and time for hunting.

Glancing around, he looked for his prey. She was here somewhere, he thought, and hopefully, it wouldn't take too long to find her. Tingling with anticipation, he could feel his groin tightening.

Hmm, who was the lucky lady tonight?

"Wanna buy me a drink?"

He turned and couldn't believe his luck. He didn't have to find her—*she* had found him. Her blonde hair was teased high, and her face was heavily painted with makeup. Trashy—just what he was looking for. She was a little older than the women he usually went for, but with her curvy body poured into that tight, red dress, he could forgive her age.

"Slut," he murmured under his breath before smiling and addressing her in the heavy Southern drawl he used while hunting, "Sure, darlin'. Order what you want, it's on me."

The woman giggled and asked the female bartender for a whiskey, neat. The man threw a twenty on the bar but avoided making eye contact with the woman behind it. The staff was so busy he doubted anyone would remember him, but it was always best to take precautions.

"My name's John," he lied loudly into his target's ear. "What's yours?"

"*Dafffne,*" she slurred before downing the whiskey in one shot.

Good, he thought with giddy eagerness—Daphne was already nice and wasted. Easy pickings. He had a flash of disappointment—she was almost too easy. Maybe next time, he'd look for someone more challenging, but for tonight, she would do. Who was he to look a gift horse in the mouth? Or, in this case, the gift whore.

After signaling for the bartender to refill the glass as he threw a few more bills on the dark oak bar, he picked up the new shot of whiskey and handed it to the slut. "Well, this just happens to be your lucky night, my lovely Daphne."

She tossed the honey-brown liquor down her throat and giggled even louder this time. Placing her hand on his chest, she took a step closer to him. "Why's that, babe?"

"Because you met me, that's why. What do you say we blow this place and go have ourselves a private party?"

"What'd you haf in mind?" The whiskey was doing its job faster than he expected. She had gone from seductive to sloshed in under fifteen seconds.

Taking a clear plastic bag from his pocket, he discreetly swung it in front of her glazed eyes until she finally focused on the tiny white pills it contained. "Oh, Johnny, you read my mind," she purred.

"Well, come on then." He nodded toward the rear door of the club.

Looking over her shoulder, she hesitated for a brief moment. "I shhhould let my frens know I'mmm leavin'."

Her tongue was getting thicker by the minute. If he didn't get her out of here soon, he'd have to carry her out, and people would definitely notice and remember that. "You'll never find them in this crowd. Come on, baby, I'll have you back in an hour... tops."

She seemed to consider it for a moment, and her gaze dropped to the bag he still held in the palm of his hand. Her body swayed toward him, and he grabbed her around the waist to prevent her from falling. "Are you shursh?"

The corners of his mouth turned up in a knowing grin. "Positive. You can trust me." With that, he led her out the back exit, quietly humming, "Luck Be a Lady," by Frank Sinatra, to himself.

Three hours later, as the bar was closing, her friends began bitching about Daphne and how she hadn't even told them she was leaving. They were just glad she wasn't their ride home.

Chapter 1

Sunday evening, Sean Malone sat on the back porch of his Uncle Dan's beach house. It was unseasonably warm for late March. The outside thermometer had reached a high of seventy-four degrees earlier in the day. Even now, with the sun almost completely set, it only felt like the low sixties. Still warm enough to sit outside for a little bit longer.

With his feet resting upon another chair, he finished the final chapter of the thriller from one of his favorite authors with the help of the porch light. He'd meant to read it when it was first released, but work had kept him busy over the past year or so, and his downtime had mainly been spent trying to catch up on his sleep. Now, he was two days into his month of accumulated vacation time, and he planned to do nothing but relax before starting his new position at the FBI office in Greenville, North Carolina. That was a little over an hour away from his uncle's cottage in Whisper on the Outer Banks, where he was staying for the next three weeks while his leased apartment was being renovated and updated. The apartment was halfway between Whisper and Greenville and a bit of a mess at the moment—the previous tenants hadn't been good housekeepers. Sean didn't mind, though, since he had the beach house all to himself. And although he was already missing the warmer Florida weather, he was happy to be near his family again.

He'd put in for a transfer from the Jacksonville, Florida, headquarters six months earlier after he found out his eldest brother, KC, and his new wife, Moriah, were expecting a baby. The child, due in three weeks, would be the first Malone of the next generation, and Sean wanted to live near them so he could be a part of his niece or nephew's life.

KC was a SEAL instructor at the Little Creek Navy Base in Virginia, ninety minutes north of Whisper, and Moriah was a substitute teacher at the local elementary school. Their middle brother, Brian, also lived near Whisper in the Elizabeth City, North Carolina, suburbs, where he worked as a special agent with the State Bureau of Investigation.

Dan Malone had raised his three nephews in the tiny beach house after their parents were killed in a plane crash when the boys were teenagers. Since then, they had grown into men and had moved on with their lives, and Dan was now living in an apartment above his hardware store in the middle of the small town. The old man was sentimental and would never sell the little cottage, keeping it so his nephews could use it whenever they wanted.

Sean glanced at his watch. Ten to six. His uncle and Bonnie Whitman were bringing dinner over in a few minutes. He was looking forward to Bonnie's famous beef stew. It wasn't often he had a home-cooked meal anymore, and the woman could cook better than anyone he knew. She had been Dan's wife's best friend since first grade and remained close to the Malone family ever since Dan was widowed at a young age.

"Sean? Are you here?"

He frowned at the strange female voice. It wasn't Bonnie—he didn't know who it was. He stood, stepped over to the porch railing, and looked down. The outside lights bathed the patio and porch in a soft, white glow. He was startled to see a beautiful blonde woman waving up at him. Her long hair was up in a ponytail, but he could tell just by looking that it was soft and silky. The striking, green eyes staring up at him were familiar, but he couldn't recall why.

When he didn't say anything immediately, the woman's mouth widened into the sexiest smile he'd seen in a long time. "You don't remember me, do you?"

"Um, I'm sorry, I don't," he responded in confusion as she climbed the stairs to where he stood.

"I'm Grace Whitman, Bonnie's niece."

Sean's eyes grew wide in shock. "Grace? Holy cow! I'mx I'm sorry, I didn't recognize you." Looking her up and down—and definitely liking what he saw—he continued. "Wow! The last time I saw you, I think you were thirteen and still dressing like a tomboy."

"And you were eighteen and running off to join the Army." She walked straight up to him and gave him a friendly hug. His breath caught at the sudden contact. "You look great."

As she stepped back, he gave her another appraising look. "So do you. I mean, look at you! I can't believe you're the same person. I remember you had short hair, skinny knees, and braces."

She grimaced, then smiled wryly. "Yeah, well, I grew up over the past fourteen years."

Boy, has she ever.

He shook his head to clear any potential dirty thoughts about her very adult body. Bonnie was family, which made her niece family too... unfortunately. "Not that I'm not glad to see you, but what are you doing here?"

"Aunt Bonnie and Dan told me to meet them here for dinner. Didn't they tell you I was coming?"

He shook his head again, this time in response to her question. "No, they didn't."

"Then that's why you look so shocked." She giggled. "I can't believe how long it's been since I've seen you. Between college and then work, I haven't been down this way often over the past few years, and whenever I did manage to come down, you were never here." She paused, then handed him the bottle of wine she was carrying. "I thought a nice merlot would go great with Aunt Bonnie's stew."

Taking the bottle, he indicated the table he had been sitting at earlier. "I'm sorry, where are my manners? Have a seat. I'll go grab a few glasses and a corkscrew."

He placed the wine on the table and hurried inside, his thoughts completely on the woman sitting on the porch.

Wow! Little Grace Whitman has grown into one hot, gorgeous lady.

He never would have expected that. The last time he saw her, she had been short, flat-chested, and all arms and legs with no hips. A little girl. But time had definitely changed her for the better. Now, fourteen years later, she was about five eight, trim, with curves in all the right places, and all woman.

Sean's adulterated thoughts were interrupted by the sound of car doors slamming. Glancing out the kitchen window, he saw his uncle and Bonnie walking up the driveway. Dan carried a large stockpot, while Bonnie held a brown paper bag with a loaf of French bread sticking out of the top. Leading the way was Dan's rescue dog, a black Labrador mix named Jinx. Grabbing four wine glasses and a corkscrew, Sean headed back out toward the deck.

Dan, Bonnie, and the dog climbed the porch steps,

and the younger Malone held the door open for them with his hip since his hands were full. The aroma from the stockpot almost brought him to his knees. It seemed like a lifetime had passed since he'd tasted Bonnie's beef stew—at least three years, he figured.

Bonnie winked at him. "I see our surprise got here before we did."

He winked back. "And a delightful surprise she was. I just wish I'd had a little warning. I'm dressed like a street bum." And he was. He glanced down, suddenly dismayed that he was wearing an old pair of jeans with holes in both knees and a wrinkled, grey T-shirt.

She gave him a quick kiss on his cheek. "Don't worry. You look fine."

Letting the door close behind the couple after they entered the cottage, he strode to where Grace was sitting. He placed the wine glasses on the table and set about opening the bottle. "So, how long are you visiting for?"

"Oh, I'm not visiting." Grace began handing him the glasses one by one for him to fill. "My move to Whisper is official as of last week."

"Really? What happened to New York? Aren't your parents still there?"

"My folks retired to Prescott, Arizona, six months ago, but I'm an east-coast girl at heart, so I decided to move down here to be closer to Aunt Bonnie." Taking the last filled glass from Sean, she leaned back in her chair and relaxed. "I'm opening my own physical therapy practice in town, hopefully in two weeks."

"That's right! Bonnie told me a few years ago that you became a physical therapist. You were working for some hospital in New York City, right?" He took the chair next to her and settled in.

"Right. Columbia Presbyterian. I was there for the past four years and got some great experience." She paused and shrugged. "But, I've always wanted to open my own place. When Mom and Dad told me they were moving to Prescott, I decided to open my PT business in Whisper. I looked into it, and there are no physical therapy clinics near here—the closest is a twenty-minute ride away. This way, people don't have to drive that far two or three times a week. I applied for my state license and got it a few months ago."

"Good for you." He held his glass out to her. "Here's to your success."

She clinked her glass with his. "Why, thank you. And from your mouth to God's ear."

"What are we toasting?" They both looked up to see Dan Malone and Jinx walking toward them.

"To Grace's new business," his nephew replied. He handed Dan one of the filled glasses.

"Well, then..." Dan raised the glass in a toast. "Here's to Grace. May she be so busy that she has to hire some help."

Grace laughed, and Sean thought he had never heard anything so beautiful. Giving himself a mental shake, he reminded himself this was Bonnie's niece. He had no business thinking of her as anything but... damn it.

"The chef sent me out to get you," Dan said. "It's a little too chilly for us old folks to eat out here, so we set the table inside." He grabbed the fourth glass of wine as Sean stood and took the now-empty bottle with him. Grace followed, and Sean opened the door for her and his uncle.

Grace grinned at him. "I see all those manners your parents and Dan drilled into you still exist."

He chuckled as he followed her inside. "Not holding a door for your elders or a woman is a mortal sin in Dan's book."

"Damn straight," Dan agreed. Spotting Bonnie coming out of the kitchen, he put the wine glasses on the dining table and ran to relieve her of the large bowl of stew she was carrying. "And not helping a lady in need is another one." He gave Sean a meaningful look. "Now go grab the salad and bread, so Bonnie can relax. She's been slaving over your dinner all day."

Sean gave his uncle a smile and a smart salute. "Yes, sir!"

The women laughed as Dan scowled at him. "Little brat," he scoffed in a tone that was nothing but affectionate for his youngest nephew.

Sean returned with a big bowl of salad and a basket of warm, sliced bread and placed them on the table.

Sitting across from Grace, he bowed his head as Dan asked for God's blessing for their meal.

As Jinx snored softly from his spot under Dan's chair, the conversation at dinner consisted mostly of Grace and Sean relating what else had happened in their lives since they'd last seen each other. Sean related how he'd received his master's degree in criminal justice while in the Army. After he was accepted into the FBI academy in Quantico, he put in for and received his honorable discharge. "I've spent my entire career, so far, in Jacksonville, Florida. But I put in for a transfer to be near my new niece or nephew."

Grace nodded as she swallowed a sip of wine. "Dan told me KC got married, and his wife is pregnant. That's great. I can't wait to meet them. I barely knew KC since he was seventeen when you all came to live with Dan, and then he took off for the Navy the following year. Since I was nine then and only here visiting Bonnie during the summers and on holidays, I knew you and Brian better."

Sean thought back to his teenage years. He'd been fourteen, and his brother Brian sixteen, when their parents were suddenly taken away from them. The couple had been flying to Hawaii to celebrate their twentieth anniversary when the plane crashed shortly after takeoff, killing all 194 souls on board. Dan, a widower with no children of his own, had taken the three boys in to finish raising them as his brother and his wife had—with rules, sternness, and much love. He may have been thrown unexpectedly into the role of parent, but Dan Malone had fully accepted the responsibility, and the boys had flourished.

Despite the tragedy in their formative years, the three boys had grown up to be respectable men, each serving in a different military branch. KC had chosen a career in the Navy, and Sean and Brian had both gone into law enforcement after stints in the Army and Air Force, respectively. Their uncle couldn't be prouder of them and always bragged about their accomplishments to anyone willing to listen.

Returning to the present, Sean told Grace, "Well, you'll see KC and Moriah in two weeks for Easter since they're coming here. Bonnie invited us all for dinner— God bless her and her fantastic cooking." He chuckled, giving the older woman a quick look filled with fondness. "You'll see Brian too. He's a special agent with the State Bureau of Investigation now and lives near Elizabeth City."

"Good for him," Grace replied, then added enthusiastically, "I can't wait to see him."

Sean silently gritted his teeth. He remembered teasing his older brother when it had been obvious that prepubescent Grace had an enormous crush on Brian. Now, though, the thought of Grace and Brian together bothered the hell out of him. Did she still have an infatuation with the middle Malone brother? He sure as hell hoped not.

The rest of the evening went by quickly but

comfortably, and Sean's guests left just after 10:00 p.m. Three hours later, he was sound asleep, having a very erotic dream about a woman who looked, not surprisingly, exactly like Grace Whitman, and she was doing incredible things to him with her mouth and hands. But for some reason, there was an annoying telephone ringing in the background of his dream. It was making it hard for him to concentrate on what his fantasy woman was doing to him.

His eyes opened, and he realized the ringing was coming from his cell phone on the nightstand beside him. Groaning at the untimely interruption and the fact that he was harder than he had been in a long time, he grabbed the phone and answered it without looking at the caller ID.

"Who the hell is this?" he growled.

There was a pause, and then, "Sean? It's Sheriff Griffin. Sorry to wake you."

"Matt?" He glanced at the bedside clock. One fifteen in the morning. A brush of fear swept over him. "What's wrong? Is it Uncle Dan?"

"No! No! Sorry, didn't mean to scare you," the sheriff apologized. "But I need your professional assistance. Dan told me you were staying at the beach house. I'm out on a homicide, and I think we have a major problem on our hands. I'd appreciate it if you could come to take a look."

Sean sat up, the last of his dream fading quickly from his head. He climbed out of bed. "Where are you?" Whatever Matt needed help with, it didn't sound good. In fact, the man actually sounded scared.

"Do you remember how to get to Red Maple Park?"

"Yeah." He pulled a clean, unripped pair of jeans from the middle drawer of the dresser.

"Well, when you get here, follow the lights." The sheriff paused again as he cleared his throat. "And Sean?"

"What?"

"I hope you have an empty stomach."

Fuck.

Chapter 2

Twenty minutes later, Sean pulled his new black Mustang into the playground parking lot. Top of the line and fully loaded, the vehicle was a gift to himself for his birthday last month, and he loved it with pure male pride. He was immediately stopped by a young sheriff's deputy he'd never met before on his visits to Whisper. The uniformed man looked more like a teenager playing dress up, yet his name tag read Deputy J.R. Peterson. Rolling down his window, Sean flashed his FBI identification. "Sheriff Griffin is expecting me."

The thin man's head bobbed up and down until Sean thought it would fly off its perch. "Yes, sir. He told me to look out for you. I'm not sure you want to drive that nice car to the crime scene, though. It's down that dirt trail." The deputy pointed to his right at a wide walking path leading into the heavy foliage.

"How far into the woods are they?"

"About a half mile, sir." Peterson appeared more impressed with Sean's ride than with being in the presence of an FBI agent, eyeing the sleek, long lines of the Mustang. The deputy was practically slobbering.

Pulling the car into a parking space, Sean popped the trunk release, then climbed out and engaged the locks, not wanting to tempt the deputy into taking a closer look. The kid would probably drool all over the gray, leather seats. He retrieved a Maglite flashlight from the trunk before slamming it shut and striding toward the trail.

After a short walk in, passing several patrol cars and two county Bureau of Criminal Investigation vans along the way, he came across another deputy, this one holding a clipboard. Again, he presented his ID. The deputy had Sean sign in to the crime scene and pointed to where the sheriff and several other men stood, although it was hard to miss them. The area was lit up with overly bright crime-scene lights.

Matt Griffin spotted him and hurried over. He looked like he'd just rolled out of bed and thrown on his sneakers, sweatpants, and T-shirt, which was covered by his department-issued navy jacket.

"Thanks for coming, Sean." He approached with his right hand extended. Griffin was in his early fifties, with salt-and-pepper hair, and was only an inch shorter than Sean's six-foot-three frame. The older man had known the Malone boys for most of their lives and was impressed the three of them had turned into such fine men after tragically losing their parents. Tom and Megan Malone would have been proud of them—their uncle sure was.

Sean shook his hand. "No problem. What's going on?"

A grim expression fell over the lawman's face. "Female homicide victim. Third one in the past three months."

Shit. "Serial?"

"Yeah, no doubt about it, but come take a look for yourself." Matt led him from the trail to the roped-off area. Several crime scene techs were marking off potential evidence on the other side of the yellow "Crime Scene—Do Not Cross" tape.

The sheriff handed Sean a pair of latex gloves and paper booties, then put them on himself. "We can walk in over here. BCI has already completed the grid search in this area."

Sean followed in the man's footsteps to where the female corpse lay supine on a pile of leaves and pine needles. They stopped about a foot away from her shoeless feet, and he took in the repulsive scene. The victim's eyes were open, bearing a look of horror glazed over by death. She was naked and spread-eagled. Ligature marks were prominent on her neck, but the thing that stood out the most was the bloody word "slut" crudely carved into her torso.

He tried to swallow the revulsion from his suddenly dry mouth. "Same as the other two?"

Matt nodded. "Yup. His signatures are exactly the same. Don't know who this one is yet, but the other two were in their twenties, blonde, and good-looking before this fucking psycho got hold of them. Coroner says the cutting was done while they were alive."

"Raped?"

"The first two weren't. Have to see what the ME says about this one."

Sean forced his eyes away from the mutilated torso and did a full head-to-toe inspection of the victim. "What's that on her forehead?"

"His other signature. A penny."

Taking a step closer, Sean squatted near the victim's head. Making sure he didn't disturb the body, he inspected the shiny coin. It was placed face up directly in the center of her forehead. Shaking his head, he stood and told Matt he'd seen enough for the moment. They silently retraced their steps out of the crime scene.

"Who found her?" Sean asked.

"A local woman walking her dogs."

His eyes narrowed. "This late?"

The older lawman shrugged. "Lives two blocks away and works the evening shift at a restaurant. Owns two pit bulls, so she's not afraid to walk the trail at night. The dogs pulled her this way—guess they smelled the body—and that's when she saw it. She was really shaken up, so I had one of the deputies take her home after she gave her statement."

Sean nodded. "Where's the coroner?"

Lifting his arm, Griffin glanced at his military-style watch. "There was a multiple-fatality accident on the expressway. Dispatch said someone was on their way here about five minutes ago.

"Listen, I know you're on vacation from the bureau before starting your new position, but I was wondering if you could get yourself assigned to us. You know the area and apparently have a great track record for solving cases."

Sean grimaced. "Uncle Dan's been bragging again, huh?"

"You got it." He leaned against one of the patrol cars. "Anyway, neither of my two lead detectives on this was available tonight. Brad Lynch is in D.C. at his son's wedding. You remember Jack Lynch, right? I think he was in your class."

"Yeah, I remember him and his dad. Last time I saw Brad, though, he was still in patrol. What's Jack doing these days?"

Griffin scratched his head. "Besides getting married? He's a doctor now. Cardiologist, I think. And from what Brad says, he's doing very well for himself."

Nodding, Sean brought the conversation back on track. "Who else do you have on this?"

"Brad's partner, Dave Farrell, but the idiot fell off a fucking ladder yesterday afternoon getting his daughter's kitten out of a tree. The kitten survived, but Dave's ankle didn't. He needs surgery and will be out for the next few weeks. Brad is back on Tuesday. In the meantime, I'm taking the lead on this until he returns. I'll call him in the morning and fill him in."

Any further conversation was interrupted by the arrival of the coroner's black van. Two men got out, and one approached the sheriff while the other walked to the rear of the van and opened the back doors.

"You're starting to make my life hell, Matt," the gray-haired coroner said as he reached them.

Griffin chuckled wryly and held out his hand. "Sorry to bother you, Pete."

"Sure you are." There was no mistaking the sarcasm as the man shook the sheriff's hand. "Who's this?" he asked curiously, tilting his head toward Sean.

"Sean Malone," Matt answered. "Special Agent with the FBI, and a friend. Sean, this is our head coroner, Dr. Peter Hansen."

The two men exchanged hellos and shook hands. Pete wasted no more time and started his inquiry. "Is it another one?"

"Yeah," Griffin replied.

"Terrific. Where do these fucking psychos come from?"

The sheriff snorted. "If I knew that, I'd be rich and famous."

Sean waited until the coroner and his assistant stepped over to the crime scene, then turned to Matt.

"Call my supervisor in the morning." He took a business card out of his wallet and asked to borrow a pen. After scribbling his new boss's name and the main office number on the back, he handed the card and pen to the sheriff. "Special Agent in Charge Clay Osbourne. He's a good guy. I worked with him in Jacksonville for a few years before he got promoted. Tell him you're requesting me and why. He might assign someone else to work with me, but since I don't know anyone else in the unit yet, your guess is as good as mine on who it'll be."

He paused and glanced back over to the buzzing crime scene. "Well, if there's nothing more for me to see, I'll head home. When should I meet you at the station? I want to go over everything you've got on the other two cases."

Running a hand through his hair, Griffin sighed heavily. "Make it noon. I won't be out of here for another hour or so, and I'm running on fumes. I'll have Pete wait for us before he starts the autopsy."

"Sounds good. See you tomorrow."

"Thanks, Sean. I appreciate whatever help you can give us."

Sean gave the older man a fist bump and started walking back toward his car. He doubted he would dream of anything except the dead woman for the rest of the night.

Shit.

Chapter 3

At ten minutes to twelve on Monday morning, Sean walked into the Dare County Sheriff's Department, located in Manteo, wearing a gray sports jacket over a black T-shirt and a pair of jeans. His weapon, holstered on his hip, was hidden by the jacket. He hadn't planned on working for another few weeks, so his suits, along with most of his personal possessions, were in a storage unit he'd rented while waiting for his apartment to be ready. He'd have to stop by and grab a few of them if he was going to be officially working the case.

He held his identification up to the bulletproof glass at the front desk for the deputy, who told him that Sheriff Griffin was already in his office waiting for him. The deputy slid a visitor's tag through a slot in the window and pressed a hidden button under the desk. A buzzing noise sounded, and he gestured for Sean to proceed through a wood and glass door a few feet to his left, which had been unlocked electronically. Halfway down the hallway on the left-hand side was the department's detective bureau, and at this time of the day, the room was brimming with activity. Some of the dozen or so detectives were at their desks, either going through reports or talking on the phone. Three others were sitting at a conference table in the middle of the room, leisurely eating deli sandwiches while discussing a case. It looked like almost every other detective bullpen Sean had ever walked into.

He strode past the unit and entered the next door on his right. The lettering on the tinted glass read Sheriff Matthew C. Griffin. The secretary's desk was empty, so he approached the door to Griffin's office and knocked. A deep "come in" was the immediate response.

Sean opened the door and found a ragged-looking Griffin, wearing his navy-blue uniform and gold shield, sitting behind a large oak desk, laden with files, paperwork, and a desktop computer. The office was large and comfortable. In addition to the desk and two upholstered guest chairs, there was a conference table surrounded by eight straight-backed chairs. Beyond the table were three six-foot-tall bookcases overflowing with law enforcement manuals and pictures of the sheriff with various dignitaries, deputies, and family members. Scattered amid all that were a variety of trophies and plaques won by, or presented to, Griffin over the years. A large flat-screen TV on the same wall as the door completed the décor.

"Welcome to my nightmare," the sheriff said wryly.

Sean stepped into the room but didn't sit. "Didn't get much sleep, did you?"

Stifling a yawn, Griffin didn't verbally answer but nodded his head.

"Neither did I."

The older man stood and stretched his back. "I spoke to your boss about an hour ago, and he said if you didn't mind taking the case, he was okay with it. Told me they're actually short-staffed at the moment, so he's glad you could help out. Also said to call him if you need more help, but for now, you're it. I'm forming a task force and contacted SBI. They'll be sending two special agents over later for a two o'clock meeting. Lynch will be the lead on this when he gets back tomorrow morning."

Sean nodded. His SAC had called him right after hanging up with the sheriff and relayed the same information about him helping out on the case. It was also common for the State Bureau of Investigations to get involved in cases like this—they had more resources than the local guys. "Okay, where do you want to go from here? Reports or autopsy?"

Grabbing a navy blue windbreaker from a hook on the wall behind him, Griffin pulled it on. "The morgue. Pete's holding the post 'til we get there. He's got a busy day and wasn't too happy about waiting."

"Lead the way."

Twenty minutes later, they were signing into the county morgue located about five miles from Griffin's office. Matt took a container of medicated vapor rub from his pocket, applied a small amount to his upper lip, and offered some to Sean. Most experienced law enforcement officers used the trick to lessen the stench of death and make it a little more tolerable. Unfortunately, there were many times, depending on the body's decomposition, when even that didn't work. Sean had never lost his stomach at a postmortem but had come close a few times. Over the years, he had seen many agents and police officers run for a trash can —even the ones who thought they were too tough to toss their cookies. It was a humbling experience for most.

A middle-aged female receptionist told them Dr. Hansen was in the autopsy suite #3. When they entered the cool, sterile examination room, they found he was just beginning the examination of their victim. He was speaking into a dictating microphone as he visually inspected the body. Switching off the recorder momentarily, he turned to the newcomers with narrowed eyes. "You're late. All the X-rays, photos, and external evidence collection are complete."

He nodded toward his female assistant. "Tess Bingham, this is Sean Malone, and you already know the sheriff."

She smiled at both of them before putting on a

mask with a clear plastic shield that would protect her face from any splatter of bodily fluids. The medical examiner eyed the men. "We're just about ready to open her. Any questions?"

The two lawmen stood about five feet away from the corpse since neither had donned any covering that would protect their clothing. Sean eyed the red slashes on the victim's torso. "Any idea what he's using to carve the lettering?"

"I'm pretty sure he's simply using a sharp utility knife, such as a Leatherman or Swiss Army. It's not precise enough to be a scalpel or crude enough for anything jagged like a steak knife."

Hansen raised his eyebrows as if to ask if there were any other questions. When Sean shook his head slightly, the coroner turned the recorder back on and put on his own protective mask. Picking up a scalpel from a nearby tray, he proceeded to make a "Y" incision from the victim's collarbones to her sternum and straight down her abdomen, exposing the inner workings of the human body.

Neither Sean nor Matt visibly reacted to the invasive procedure since they had both watched their fair share of autopsies, but it didn't mean they weren't affected by it. No one should have to suffer the indignity of being naked on a cold slab as their insides are exposed and examined to determine the cause of death. The worst part came when Tess started up the bone saw and began to cut through the ribs so they could be temporarily removed from the upper torso. This was done so they could remove the lungs and heart to be weighed and given a thorough examination. Small cross-sections of the organs would also be taken for further analysis if needed. The rest would be placed back inside the chest cavity for the victim's burial.

The same saw would then be used on the victim's skull to expose the brain, and the process would be repeated for that organ. Sean thought the grinding noise was a hundred times worse than a dentist's drill and always found it very unsettling.

At the end of the extensive autopsy, the results were what they had expected and then some. Death by ligature strangulation. The killer had slowly drained the victim's life from her body... several times. Hansen reported, "It appears, this time, the killer choked her until she was no longer breathing, then revived her to do it again and again. He's evolving—fine-tuning his craft as he goes, which I would expect from a serial."

Griffin grimaced and murmured, "Bastard."

Sean asked, "Can you tell how many times?"

"My guess is three or four. Some of the ligature marks overlap, so it's difficult to tell, but no more than five times. As with the other two vics, there's no trace evidence of what he used, but my guess is a scarf or something similar. Some marks look like they came from creases in the fabric." He pointed to the victim's limbs. "There are also ligature marks on her wrists and ankles, so she was tied up too. The empty stomach and acid irritation in the esophagus indicate she vomited at some point, but I don't know if that was before or during the attack. The drug toxicology reports will take several days, but her blood alcohol level was point-three-oh percent."

"Jeez. That's almost four times the legal driving limit." Sean stared at the body on the table. "She was drunk as a skunk."

Griffin shook his head. "Hopefully, she was passed out for most of the attack."

"Oh, by the way," the pathologist added. "We managed to get a skin-cell sample from under two of her fingernails. Looks like she might have scratched the guy."

The sheriff's eyes widened. This had been an unexpected lead. "Really?"

"Yup. Sent it upstairs to the lab already."

After thanking Hansen for waiting for them, Matt and Sean took the elevator two floors up from the morgue to where trained technicians were scrutinizing all the physical evidence found at the scene and on the body. The head of the county's criminal investigation lab, Hank Cunningham, stood just inside the department's door, reading through a file when they walked in. His eyes lit up upon seeing the sheriff. "Oh, good, you're here. I was just about to call you."

After introducing the man to Sean, Matt asked, "You got something for us?"

"Yup. Managed to get a print off the penny this time. Ran it through AFIS and got a hit."

Griffin couldn't hide his excited surprise. "You're kidding? Please don't tell me it's to an unsolved crime with no name attached."

"No, we actually got lucky for once." He handed over a printed report.

Sean read from the page over the sheriff's shoulder. "Stuart Crowell. Twenty-five years old. Petty larceny and burglary. Spent two years in the Virginia State prison system. No parole violations and hasn't missed a meeting with his probation officer since his release six months ago."

"Doesn't exactly sound like a serial killer, does he?" the sheriff asked no one in particular.

"Still need to check him out, though. Unfortunately, his print could have ended up on that penny anywhere." Sean sighed heavily. He had a feeling the lead wouldn't pan out—investigations in extreme crimes like this were never that simple—but they still had to follow up on it. He looked at Cunningham. "Anything else? Was her clothing found?"

"Nope."

Matt glanced up from the report. "We didn't find the other women's clothes, either. He's dumping them somewhere else or keeping them as trophies. And we haven't found the kill sites yet. None of them were killed where they were found." Addressing Hank again, he asked, "Did you get a chance to run our vic's prints?"

The technician shook his head. "Nothing in AFIS or any other government database. She's never been fingerprinted for any reason."

"So she's still a Jane Doe for now. Shit."

"We're still processing trace evidence from the body and the scene, including the fingernail scrapings, but nothing else appears out of the ordinary right now. Except, of course, for the penny and body carving. I'll call you if we find anything."

"How long for the DNA from the scrapings?" Griffin asked.

"I sent a sample up to the state lab and asked for it to be a top priority, but it'll still take weeks." Cunningham held up his hand at the sheriff's scowl. "And before you ask, yes, that's the fastest they can do it."

Griffin wasn't happy about that, but he nodded anyway.

"Did you save any samples?" Sean asked.

Cunningham nodded. "Yes, I always hold some back in case the sample is lost."

"If you send it to the FBI lab, we might be able to get it back faster. I'll have my SAC call and put a rush on it."

"That'd be great. I'll fill out the forms and overnight everything before I leave."

Sean pulled out one of his business cards and jotted down his cell number. "Here's my number if you need me. What's the number here? I'll call you when I have a contact name for you to address the samples to. That way, they don't get tossed into a long-term waiting bin.

The head tech grabbed a nearby notepad and wrote down the lab's phone number and extension. The two men were about to leave when Sean stopped and asked, "What year was the penny?"

Cunningham's eyebrows shot up in surprise, then he loudly repeated the question to a young male technician across the room.

"1993," was the reply. "Same as the other two."

Matt eyed Sean. "What're you thinking?"

"I don't know yet. Were the other two in the same condition?"

"Yes." It was Cunningham who responded.

Sean let the info spin around his mind a few times. "It's a little odd that they all had the same year and seem pretty clean, despite their age. They've been in circulation for what? Well over twenty years? Maybe the year means something to the killer."

Obviously, following the Fed's train of thought, Cunningham nodded in agreement. "I'll have my techs run a few tests to see if anything was used to clean them up, but I have a jar of change sitting at home. There are plenty of older coins that look shiny, while newer ones look old. Depends on who had their grubby little hands on them."

Thanking the head tech, the two men left. On the way to the parking lot, Griffin called dispatch on his cell phone and told them to have deputies track down Stuart Crowell for questioning. The dispatcher informed him that two SBI agents were waiting for him at the station. "Tell them I'll be there in twenty minutes. By the way, who'd they send?"

The sheriff smiled as he hung up the phone. "Well, it looks like I got lucky."

"How's that?" Sean asked.

"Not only do I have Sean Malone, the famous FBI agent, on the case, but I have his brother Brian Malone, one of North Carolina's finest special agents."

Sean grinned for the first time all day. "The Malone brothers ride again. Yee-haw!"

After making a quick stop at a deli for a takeout lunch, they headed back to the station, where they entered through a side door with Griffin's passkey and commandeered a conference room. The sheriff immediately left the room again, hurried into his office, and then brought back the files from the two previous homicides, as well as the thin file he had started on the current victim. Within days, it would probably be as thick as the others.

Just as they were getting ready to sit at the large table, Brian Malone entered the room along with a man in his early thirties. Both were dressed in sports coats, ties, and khakis. Sean's brother stood six feet three, while the other man was about two inches shorter and a tad broader. Brian introduced his partner to the sheriff. "Matt Griffin, Rafael Montoya."

As the sheriff shook his hand, Montoya added, "Call me Rafe."

"Nice to meet you, Rafe. Feel free to call me Matt."

Montoya nodded, then turned to Sean as Brian said, "And this guy is the sorriest son of a bitch you'll ever meet."

Sean gave his brother a playful but hard punch on his left shoulder. "Yeah, well, I can honestly say you taught me everything I know." He extended his hand to the other agent. "Sean Malone."

Montoya shook the offered hand. "Nice to finally meet you. Brian's always talking about you, KC, and your uncle."

"Ha! Proof that he loves me."

Brian pointed at his brother. "What he didn't say is that I'm always trashing you."

He smiled. "That I believe. But ya still love me." When Brian opened his mouth to argue, Sean quickly held up a hand and stopped him. "Don't deny it, or you won't get the sandwiches we brought for you."

His grin widened when his older brother glared at him quietly. Everyone knew the way to control Brian was with food. The man could eat nonstop, yet was one of the fittest guys in the SBI, thanks to his longtime discipline of running every morning.

The sheriff left the room to attend a brief meeting on his schedule, while the three other men sat down at the table and spread out their lunches and the case files. Brian began scanning through several reports while he ate. Sean, on the other hand, preferred to finish eating before reading. He knew he would lose his appetite if he examined the details of the cases during lunch. It had taken almost a full hour since the autopsy for his stomach to settle.

They ate in silence for several minutes. When Montoya got up to use the men's room, Sean eyed his brother. "Did you know Bonnie's niece is in town?"

Brian didn't look up from the file but answered absently, "Little Gracie? Dan mentioned she moved here, but I haven't seen her yet."

He felt relief at his brother's nonchalance. Hopefully, Brian wouldn't be interested in Grace because the more Sean thought about her, the more he wanted to see her again. And soon. "She came over last night for dinner with Bonnie and Dan."

Brian lifted his gaze from the report. "Yeah? She still gawky looking?"

"Um, not really." Mentally kicked himself, Sean knew he should have kept his mouth shut.

His reluctance to elaborate didn't go unnoticed. "What does 'not really' mean? Don't tell me she's hot."

Hot didn't begin to describe Grace—she was downright gorgeous. Calling her hot was like saying an erupting volcano was a campfire. Sean shrugged, grabbed one of the files, and pretended to be suddenly engrossed in it. But Brian wasn't buying it. "Uncle Dan said she was opening her own PT practice. Maybe I'll go see her for my back pain."

Sean's head whipped up, and his eyes narrowed at his brother. "What fucking back pain?"

"The pain I just got," Brian teased, dramatically shrugging his shoulders. "I could go for a good back massage."

The younger Malone growled to himself. If he could, he would have kicked himself in the ass. Now that Brian knew he was interested in Grace Whitman, his brother was going to drive him nuts. They'd always had a healthy rivalry when it came to women. "Can we get back to the case, asshole?"

An evil grin spread across Brian's face as he crumpled up the paper his sandwich had been wrapped in and tossed it like a basketball into the garbage can in the corner of the room. Grabbing his lower back, he moaned loudly. Sean wanted to kill the asshole right then and there.

A half-hour later, the three men were elbow-deep in the case files, each making notes on pads of white, legal-size paper. They all glanced up when the conference room door opened. A young, dark-haired deputy whose name tag read "Montgomery" stepped in. "The sheriff told me to tell you we got a missing person call that sounds like it might be last night's homicide. Name's Daphne Jones. He thought you'd want to check it out since he's still stuck in the budget meeting." He handed Sean a piece of paper. "Larry

Cumberland's at the residence now, taking the initial report. He said her picture matches the description. I'm Ned Montgomery, by the way."

"Special Agent Sean Malone. This is my brother, Brian, and Rafe Montoya with SBI," Sean said as he stood and shook the deputy's proffered hand. "How long has she been missing?"

"Last seen by her roommate on Saturday night. Her friends thought she'd left them at some club. Supposedly, no one's seen her since."

Brian's gaze went to his brother and then his partner. "Who's coming with me?"

Montoya shrugged his shoulders. "Doesn't matter to me, but I'd rather keep reviewing the other two cases. You can fill me in later."

Grabbing his discarded sports jacket from the back of his chair, Sean nodded. "That's fine with me." He stopped Montgomery before the deputy had a chance to step out of the room. "Do you know if patrol has located Stuart Crowell?"

"Not yet. But I'm the desk deputy until 2000 hours, so I'll call you as soon as I hear anything."

Sean gave the deputy his cell phone number and then followed his brother out the door.

Within twenty-five minutes, they were sitting at the kitchen table in a two-bedroom apartment in nearby Kitty Hawk, talking to Cheryl Armstrong. The top-floor unit was one of six occupying a three-floor walk-up in the town, which was part of Dare County.

Several pictures provided by Cheryl led them to believe their victim was her roommate, thirty-two-year-old Daphne Jones, a receptionist at a local insurance agency. A comparison of her dental records would confirm it, but Sean was certain the results would match. They'd gotten a brief report from Deputy Cumberland, but the brothers wanted the woman to start from the beginning. But before that, they had to fill her in on how her roommate had died. Cumberland hadn't disclosed the details yet.

Hating this part of the job, Sean squatted next to Cheryl's chair when she asked to know what had happened for the third time since they'd arrived moments ago. "I'm sorry to tell you this, but Daphne was murdered."

Cheryl gasped, her eyes filled with horror. Before she could ask any questions he couldn't answer, he continued. "I can't give you the details at the moment, but we need your help to find out who did this to her. Okay?"

Her hand covered her mouth as tears began to roll down her cheeks, but she nodded her assent. Brian sat in a chair across from her at the small table, with a notepad to jot things down, while Sean stood and leaned against the nearby counter, taking the lead. "I know you've already told the deputy what happened, but I'd appreciate it if you repeated everything to us. Sometimes people remember things they didn't think of the first time they tell their story."

Cheryl took a deep breath as she wiped her teary eyes with a tissue Deputy Cumberland had silently handed her. "A b-bunch of us girls went out Saturday night. We-we went to dinner at Martino's in-in Jarvisburg. It's a new r-restaurant on Central Avenue."

"What time was that?"

Clearing her throat, she got her stuttering under control. "About six thirty. I drove Daphne and our friend Janet, and we met Diane and Michelle there. We were there until around nine, then went to Visions, that nightclub in Elizabeth City." She looked at Brian and then Sean to see if they knew the bar.

"I'm familiar with the place," Brian said, gesturing with his hand for her to continue.

"The place was packed as usual, and we were all running into people we knew. It wasn't anything new to lose track of one another for a while, you know?"

He nodded. "Go on. When did you realize Daphne was missing?"

Cheryl sniffed several times before answering. "We honestly didn't think she was missing. We just figured she met a guy and ditched us. It wouldn't have been the first time... but she wasn't a slut or anything. She didn't do it a lot, just every once in a while."

Both Brian and Sean winced slightly at Cheryl's use of the word "slut." The sheriff hadn't revealed to anyone outside the department what had been carved into the victims' torsos.

Brian made some notes on his pad. "Okay. When

was the last time anyone saw her, and when did you notice she was gone?"

"Um... the last time I saw her was about eleven, I think—we were in the ladies' room together. Around one-thirty or so, the rest of us started to look for her because Janet had had too much to drink and wanted to go home. We searched the whole place and couldn't find Daphne. At two-thirty, the bar was closing, so we figured she'd hooked up with someone and left."

"Why didn't you report her missing when she didn't come home yesterday?" Sean asked.

Her gaze went to his, and she shook her head. "I didn't know she didn't come home. When I got up, her bedroom door was shut, so I figured she was sleeping. I spent most of the day babysitting my nieces while my brother and sister-in-law went to a wedding. When I got home, I went straight to bed. It wasn't until ten this morning when her boss called to find out why she wasn't at work that I realized she was missing."

After asking a few more questions about Daphne's routine, ex-boyfriends, and whether or not she'd reported seeing anything or anyone out of the ordinary lately, Brian finished by inquiring, "Does she have family in the area? We're going to have to contact them."

"Her family's in Chicago. She has no relatives near here. Their address and phone number are in her journal on her dresser. She told me if anything ever...

ever happened to her, th-those were the people I should contact."

She pointed to Daphne's bedroom. As Deputy Cumberland went to retrieve the book, the reality of her roommate's murder finally hit, and Cheryl began to sob loudly. "Oh, my God. I can't believe she's dead. We should have looked for her."

Sean placed a comforting hand on the distraught woman's shoulder and spoke in a soft, reassuring tone. "Your friend was probably far away by the time anyone realized she was missing. None of this is your fault. Place all the blame on the person who killed her." As Cheryl looked up at him with red eyes, he continued. "And I promise you, we'll do everything we can to find Daphne's killer and give her justice."

Chapter 4

Sean, Brian, and Montoya left the Sheriff's Department a little after 6:00 p.m. and parted ways. There was still no word on Stuart Crowell, so they had spent the rest of the afternoon interviewing the women Daphne Jones had been with on Saturday night. No one saw who she'd left with. The nightclub, Visions, didn't open until eight o'clock, so Brian had asked dispatch to assign a detective to interview the staff and find out if they had video surveillance of the place. They would follow up on the information in the morning.

The sheriff had called from his drawn-out budget meeting and ordered the task force to meet the following morning. He wanted a report from the detectives and the crime scene techs at 9:00 a.m. Detective Brad Lynch would be back by then and needed to be updated. The team would brainstorm about where to go from there.

As he drove through the small business district of Whisper, Sean noticed the lights were on in the store-front across from his uncle's hardware store. Grace had mentioned that it was where her new business was located. She'd been lucky the owner of a former yoga and Pilates studio had closed up shop and moved south, leaving the prime location available.

On a whim, he pulled into an open parking space in front of the shop and killed the car's engine. Through the large, plate-glass window, he saw Grace painting something on one of the interior walls. Telling himself he was just being friendly by stopping in to see her new place, he climbed out of his vehicle and strode to the door. Pulling on the handle, he found it locked. When he glanced up, Grace was smiling at him and hurrying over to let him in.

Unlocking the door, she held it open for him. "Hi there. Come on in." She engaged the lock again after he entered. "Welcome to Pro-Care Physical Therapy."

Sean chuckled as she turned toward him. "You've got paint on your nose."

"Oops. Thanks." She pulled a rag from the rear pocket of her jeans and wiped the small splotch of gray paint from her face. "Did I get it?"

"All gone."

Stepping further into the studio, he took in the newly carpeted floor and painted room. Grace was in the process of adding large, gray silhouettes on the pale blue walls. Each was shaped like a male or female athlete performing different sports. The tiny reception area had a built-in desk and was separated from the large space by a half-wall, which housed the remainder of the business. Both rooms were void of any furniture or equipment. He turned back to Grace. "It looks fantastic but a little sparse."

She giggled and rolled her eyes. "Obviously, my furniture and equipment haven't been delivered yet. The reception chairs, PT tables, and a stacked washer/dryer are being delivered on Thursday. The gym apparatus comes next Monday, and the machinery later in the week."

"That's a lot of stuff." He followed her back to where she'd been working.

"It is. I was able to buy everything but the medical equipment with the loan I took out. The rest is rented." She sighed. "Hopefully, I'll be able to buy them, too, after a year or so."

"Will you be working here alone?" he asked.

Grace shook her head. "No. I've already hired a receptionist and a part-time billing clerk for now, and I put an ad in the county paper yesterday for another PT. I received a few responses today and set up a couple of interviews. Tomorrow I'm going around to some of the doctors' offices in the area to introduce myself and try to drum up some business. If all goes well, I can open on time."

"That's great." Sean could see the pride in her eyes. They glittered with excitement, and he wondered what they would look like in the throes of passion. God, he had to stop thinking like that. She was practically family... yet she wasn't, was she?

Picking up her paintbrush again, she turned back to finish painting the outline of a golfer. "So what brings you by?"

"I... uh, was over at the Sheriff's Department with Matt Griffin and my brother Brian. Matt asked us to help out on a case. I saw your light on as I was heading home." He felt funny just standing there while she worked. "Can I help you?"

"No, thanks. I'm almost done for the night. My arm's getting tired."

He laughed and came close to offering to massage it for her. He stopped himself, though, because he wasn't sure how she would take the suggestion. "Listen, have you eaten yet? I'm starved. While you finish up, I can run over to Basil's and pick up a pizza for us."

"That sounds fantastic. Their pizza is the best. I haven't had a chance to eat there since I've been back, and I'm starting to crave it!"

"Toppings?"

Her eyes lit up as she glanced over her shoulder at him. "Pepperoni, of course. Lots of it!"

Nodding, he pivoted toward the door. "Works for me. I'll be back in a few."

"Don't forget to grab some paper plates and napkins."

Sean acknowledged her with a wave over his shoulder as he unlocked the front door and let himself out. While he was gone, Grace finished the silhouette and then cleaned the paintbrushes and her hands. A short time later, they were sitting on the floor of her business with their backs against one of the walls that had been painted a few days earlier. The partially eaten pizza sat in an open box between them, along with two small bottles of Coke. Hungry, they ate in silence for a few minutes.

Reaching for a second slice, Grace asked, "So what case are you working on? No offense, but I assume it can't be good if you were asked to get involved."

He waited until he swallowed a mouthful of pizza before he answered. "No, it isn't. It's a homicide. Female victim under strange circumstances." He didn't go into it any further since it still wasn't public knowledge that a serial killer had settled into Dare County.

She looked over at him. "You can't tell me anything more, can you?"

"Not really," he admitted while grabbing a third slice. He hadn't been kidding earlier when he'd said he was starving. At least the pizza was settling better in his stomach than his sandwich had after the autopsy. "Sorry."

"No problem. I had quite a few friends on the New York police force. They couldn't discuss their cases much either." She put down her paper plate and picked up her soda bottle. "That was delicious. Thanks for getting dinner."

"No problem." He pointed to the golfer's silhouette. "The walls look great. You're a good artist."

Grace let out a small snort. "Actually, I'm a good tracer. I borrowed an old overhead projector from the elementary school, put outlines of athletes on it, and blew them up onto the wall. All I had to do was trace the images."

Looking at an empty space on the wall next to the skier, Sean was barely able to make out a pencil outline of a baseball player holding a bat. "Well, it's much better than I can do, so I'm still impressed."

She smiled at him in thanks, and he felt warm inside. Without thinking, he reached over and gently tugged a strand of her hair through his fingers. It was as silky as it looked, and he felt his groin tighten. When he realized she was staring at him questioningly, he snatched his hand back. "Sorry. You had some paint in your hair."

It was getting harder and harder to fight his attraction to her, but he was still up in the air about whether to make that attraction known. He had no idea whether she shared his feelings. Sean jumped to his feet and began to gather up the remnants of their meal. "I'd better get going. It's been a long day. I'll throw this in the dumpster out back."

Grace stood also. "I'm exhausted myself. Probably

sleep like the dead tonight." She immediately grimaced. "Sorry. Bad analogy."

"No problem. I've heard worse." Members of law enforcement tended to have a warped sense of humor. "If you're ready to leave, I'll walk you out."

"Okay. Let me just grab my purse, and I'll lock up while you take out the garbage."

Later that night, Sean lay in bed, frustrated. As tired as he was, he just couldn't shut down his racing mind. He had brought home copies of the case files to continue familiarizing himself with the facts and, hopefully, to develop a profile of the UNSUB. He'd struggled to concentrate on the computer printouts, but his attention kept wandering back to Grace.

What would she say if he invited her out on a date? He groaned. *Fuck! What would Bonnie say?* It would probably be just plain awkward for everybody. Besides, Grace probably thought of him as a brother or cousin. If he asked her out, it would undoubtedly have an *ick factor*.

He let out a loud sigh, which seemed to echo through the bedroom as he tried to recall the last time he'd had sex. If he couldn't remember, it was definitely too long ago. Maybe that's why he was suddenly interested in Grace. He rarely dated a woman for more than a few dates. After one or two nights of mutually satisfying sex, the woman usually moved on, which was fine with him.

But Grace wasn't one-night stand material. Not

even two nights. Grace Whitman was a long-term relationship woman, and Sean didn't do long-term. Hell, he barely did short-term. The longest relationship he'd had in the past five years had lasted a few days over two months before the woman had gotten tired of competing with his job. Not many women appreciated their dates being constantly interrupted by phone calls he had to take or being canceled altogether because Sean had to respond to a crime scene.

He sighed again and went back to the case reports. An hour later, his mind and body succumbed to overwhelming drowsiness, tumbling him into some much-needed sleep with the files scattered around him. He hoped he would dream of Grace and not dead bodies.

Miles away, Grace tossed and turned on her own bed. Groaning, she fluffed her pillow for the fourth time and tried again to get comfortable. Glancing around the moonlit room, she made a mental list of everything she still had to do to make her condo a home. Her first few nights in North Carolina had been spent at Bonnie's house. She then found the spacious two-bedroom unit after rejecting three other locations her realtor had suggested. Because of the loan she'd taken out for her business, she had to settle for renting the condo. The realtor told her the owners might be interested in selling the unit in the future, so a "rent with the option to buy" clause had been added to the contract.

The five-year-old complex called Hidden Cove Condominiums was in the small town of Gandy—a fifteen-minute drive to Whisper. In the middle of the six buildings, with a total of forty-eight units, was a large man-made lake and a small park with a children's playground. There was also a residents-only swimming pool on the property. The landscaping was beautiful, and Grace had instantly fallen in love with the comfortable neighborhood. After touring the condo, she informed the realtor she didn't need to see any more listings and put down a deposit. The moving company she'd used to transport her belongings from New York had stored the items until she could locate a new place. The condo had been available immediately, and she'd moved in after her furniture and boxes were delivered three days later.

The movers had placed all the large furniture exactly where she wanted it, but otherwise, the rooms were undecorated. All her belongings were still packed in moving boxes stacked against the walls in every room. Aunt Bonnie had come over the day after Grace moved in to help her unpack her kitchen and bathroom necessities, along with a few boxes of clothes. Other than that, Grace wanted to postpone the rest of the unpacking and decorating until after her business was ready to go. She'd deal with the boring white walls for now. Getting Pro-Care up and running was her main priority—everything else would just have to wait.

After flipping from her left side to her right and back again, she flung the sheets off and climbed out of bed. Maybe a warm glass of milk would help. She trudged out to the kitchen, grabbed the milk from the refrigerator, found a small saucepan to put it in, and set it on the stove to heat up. As she waited for the white liquid to warm, her thoughts returned to her impromptu dinner with Sean.

When she was younger, she'd had a huge crush on Brian Malone, but by the time she was in junior high school, Sean had gotten taller, broader, and cuter than he'd been a few years earlier. The Army had taken the boy she'd known and made him a man, and she suddenly found her infatuation shifting from the old Brian to the new Sean.

All the Malone brothers were handsome. At a young age, she'd figured out that very few girls, and then women, were immune to their looks and magnetism. Mothers found their polite and charming personalities appealing, yet every father could see through to the bad boys and free spirits hiding just below the surface.

Even though she only saw them at Thanksgiving, Easter, and a few weeks over the summer each year as a child, Grace had been close enough to the brothers back then to make some of the local girls jealous. Not that she had cared. She even remembered rubbing their noses in it a few times when she got the chance, like wrapping her hand around Brian or Sean's arms when the popular girls were around or hopping on their backs for a piggyback ride.

Looking back, her behavior had been so childish, but the boys never complained and treated her like a little sister they didn't mind hanging out with. But as they got older and started dating, Grace was the one to be jealous of being left behind, especially after she heard Sean had taken that bitchy snob Mary Jo Schreiber to the senior prom. It wasn't as if he could have taken Grace since she'd lived in New York, but she'd still been disappointed at the time.

However, now she was back in the area to stay, and her eyes were once again drawn to Sean. But this time, it was as a woman, not a pubescent girl who didn't know what real male desirability was. His rich, brown eyes seemed to change shades depending on what color shirt he was wearing, and his light brown hair was just long enough to make her yearn to run her fingers through it. The first night she saw him, it had looked as if he hadn't shaved for a day or two, but this evening, just a hint of a five o'clock shadow had covered his jawline and upper lip. She couldn't decide which was a better look on him—either way was very sexy.

Was she fascinated with him due to her childhood crush, or was this the real thing she felt? Unfortunately, Sean probably still considered her Bonnie's niece, "Little Gracie." She wondered if there was a way to get him to notice her as a woman—a woman who was very attracted to him.

A sizzling sound jerked her out of her daydream just in time to remove the milk from the stove and prevent scalding. Pouring the liquid into a coffee cup, Grace took the drink back to bed with her, and a short time later, she was finally asleep.

Chapter 5

The two Malone brothers and Rafe all arrived at the sheriff's department at eight o'clock the next morning. Sean climbed out of his car and approached the other men as they stood at the far end of the parking lot, staring at the crowd gathered at the main entrance. Multiple news vans occupied the lot as cameramen and reporters littered the front walkway of the building.

"This can't be good," Sean murmured.

Brian rolled his eyes. "You think? Let's just hope it has nothing to do with our serial."

"Twenty bucks says it does," Rafe dared.

His partner snorted. "Even I'm not crazy enough to take that bet. And speaking of which, you still owe me twenty from the game the other night."

"Yeah, I'll get right on that. I forgot to roll my loose change for you."

"Asshole. Don't laugh, Sean, but this jackass did that to me once," Brian complained. "Paid his fucking fifty-dollar bet in dimes, nickels, and pennies."

Sean shook his head. The two of them sound more like an old married couple than coworkers. But the thought of pennies had his mind going back to the case, and it was hard to laugh while thinking about that.

The lawmen managed to make their way through the chaos unnoticed. Although Sean was dressed in a dark suit, and the other men were in sports coats with their weapons and badges concealed, leaving no outward sign they were in law enforcement. As a result, the press didn't question them as they entered the station. Showing their IDs to the deputy at the front desk, they were buzzed into the back hallway and went straight to Griffin's office. His secretary, Nancy Kessler, was simultaneously talking on the phone and writing on a memo pad when they entered the reception area. Her husband taught history at the local high school and had coached both Brian and Sean in football when they were younger. Nancy recognized the brothers immediately, smiled, and gestured for the men to take seats for a moment.

The sheriff's door was closed, but they could hear him yelling through the frosted glass. "I want to know who the fucking leak is, and I want to know now! All hell is breaking loose out there, and we're no closer to finding this son of a bitch than we were two months ago. I've got every goddamned politician in Dare

County demanding answers, and I've got nothing for them.

"Brooks, I want you to pass the word that no one... I repeat... *no one* is to talk to the press about this case without my permission. And, Dworski, since every pain-in-the-ass reporter and news station in the area is outside, you might as well make a statement."

Another male voice responded, "What do you want me to say? Or not say?"

"Say we have three homicides that *may* be related. We've formed a task force that includes state and federal agents. Everything possible is being done to catch this bastard. No specific details about the murders. The pennies and the carvings are to be kept under wraps. Tell them we've stepped up patrols, women should take extra precautions, yada, yada. You know the fucking routine."

"Yes, sir."

"You can also tell them we'll be holding daily press conferences at 11:00 a.m. starting tomorrow. If we do that, hopefully, that'll stop some of those reporters from snooping around. I doubt it, but it's worth a shot." The man paused. "And if I catch *anyone* from this department talking to *any* reporter without permission, even if it's the damn maintenance staff, I swear there'll be hell to pay. They'll be cleaning every patrol car and piece of equipment with a goddamned toothbrush for the next three years. Dismissed."

The door opened suddenly, and two uniformed

captains exited the office, followed by the sheriff. "Nancy, hold my calls for the next hour or so unless it's an emergency. I've got a pounding headache."

His secretary nodded, the phone's receiver still held to her ear. She opened the top drawer of her desk and handed her boss a bottle of ibuprofen. Griffin grunted his thanks as he took it from her before turning to the three men waiting for him. "I was wondering when the damn press was going to come knocking. Come on in, guys. Join the party."

Entering the office, they found another man sitting at the conference table. He stood as they approached, and Sean immediately recognized him as Jack Lynch's father.

Griffin introduced all of them. "Brad Lynch, you already know Brian and Sean Malone, and this is Rafe Montoya, also from the SBI."

The men all shook the detective's hand, and then Brad grinned at Brian. "Hey, nice drug bust a few weeks ago."

Sean knew he was referring to a huge bust that'd gone down that had included Brian, a team from the state police, and some DEA agents. They'd taken a million dollars' worth of marijuana, cocaine, and ecstasy off the streets.

Brian nodded his thanks as Brad addressed Sean. "Good to see you again. It's been a long time."

He nodded. "At least five years. How've you been?"

"Good, good. Just got back from Jack's wedding."

"I heard. Give him my congratulations."

"I will." They all sat around the conference table. "Your Uncle Dan told me you were moving back here."

"Took a post in Greenville to be closer to the family."

"Yeah, he also told me KC and his wife are expecting. That's great."

From his seat at the head of the table, Sheriff Griffin cleared his throat. "Gentlemen, you can catch up with each other later. Let's get through this so that I can get rid of you and this fucking headache at the same time."

Brian tossed his notepad on the table in front of him. "How bad is the leak?"

Scowling, Matt ran a hand down his face. "I'm not sure. The press doesn't seem to know many details, but somehow they got a hold of the victims' names and where they were dumped."

"Shit," Montoya murmured.

That was putting it mildly. It was obvious from the sheriff's expression and demeanor that when he found the leak, he was going to plug it... permanently. Whoever was spouting information was potentially jeopardizing a conviction if an arrest were ever made. "I agree. Anyway, let's get this show on the road. Brad?"

The lead detective recapped for everyone what they knew about the first two murders. "Two months ago, Becky Travis, twenty-two, left a friend's party after drinking almost half a bottle of vodka by herself. She apparently did a disappearing act on them without saying goodbye and was walking home, which was three blocks away. From what we can tell, she never made it. Two days later, she was found in an alley in Kitty Hawk by sanitation workers. Naked, with ligature strangulation, 'slut' carved into her torso, and a penny on her forehead. No witnesses. Videos from local businesses were scarce and revealed nothing that seemed out of the ordinary.

"Three weeks ago, Shannon Emerson, twenty-four, was at a bachelorette party at a place called The Toy Box in Elizabeth City. They have a male strip show at nine—get the girls all hot and bothered—then open the place up to men at ten thirty. Her friends never saw her leave. Apparently, everyone was pretty toasted and didn't realize she was gone until around one a.m. She was supposed to be the ride home for two of the other women. Her car was still in the parking lot."

"Any surveillance video?" Montoya asked.

Lynch shook his head. "The video from inside is black and white and very grainy. We were able to pick her out a few times, but she was still with her friends at that point. After it got crowded in there, it was hard to tell one person from another. The outside cameras hadn't been working for weeks, and management hadn't gotten around to fixing them.

"Anyway, the vic was found at the edge of a

wooded area next to the soccer field of Manteo High School. The gardener was mowing the grass and spotted the body an hour before students arrived, so we were able to isolate the area. Her condition was the same as the other one. No clothes were recovered from either scene, but from photos taken at both parties, the vics were dressed to impress. We checked out the ex-boyfriends of both women and didn't come up with any leads. Neither one told family or friends about any stalkers or problems with anyone. And as far as we can tell, their lives didn't intersect with each other."

Sean took over from there, giving the two detectives the information on the latest homicide and what they'd uncovered about the victim so far. "It sounds like he's going after blonde party girls. Daphne was all dressed up, too, according to her roommate. Also, no stalkers. Her last steady boyfriend was a year ago. It ended amicably when he moved to California for business. No other leads yet. It's possible these women were just in the wrong place at the wrong time. Victims of opportunity."

He paused, then added, "I'm curious about the dump sites. The first two were left in places where they would be found relatively fast. But Daphne was left in a wooded area. If it weren't for the dogs, she wouldn't have been easily spotted from the trail. It could mean something or absolutely nothing."

Griffin reported that they still hadn't located Stuart Crowell, but patrols were actively looking for him.

"What are the chances he's our killer?" he asked, directing his question to the federal agent.

Flipping his hand in a "who knows" gesture, Sean frowned. "Slim. He doesn't really fit the profile of a serial killer, but we have to rule him out. His print could have ended up on the penny anywhere. The other pennies had smudges, nothing to confirm he'd handled them." Hank Cunningham had called him late yesterday afternoon with that information. The pennies hadn't been cleaned with anything they could detect, either.

"So, where do we go from here?" Montoya asked.

Leaning forward, Brad rested his arms on the table. He was in charge of the task force, so he'd dole out the assignments. While a federal or state agent would usually head the team, both Sean and Brian were comfortable ceding command to the man they'd known and respected for years. "We've got the surveillance tapes from Visions—I'll review those with our video expert. Each camera angle is on a different disk, so it'll take most of the day."

Sean handed the lead detective a photo of Daphne Jones. "Her roommate gave me this. She took it at the restaurant the night Daphne disappeared. It'll help you find her on the video."

Brad nodded and added the photo to the folder in front of him. "Sean, can you patch into the FBI database and see if there are any similar homicides in any other states? It'll be faster than putting in a formal request."

"Consider it done. My laptop's in the car."

"And maybe start working on a profile of our UNSUB," the detective added. "Brian and Rafe, why don't you guys check with BCI to see if Hank has anything new for us? Detective Vic Emory stopped by Vision's for us last night and compiled a list of employees who were working on Saturday night, along with their contact information. When you're done talking to Hank, getting their statements is all yours."

Brad rattled off his cell and office phone numbers for the others and then took down their contact information. "Keep in touch. We'll meet back here... say around five for a roundup. By then, it'll be on every news station, so get ready for the stampede of crazies, psychics, and general 'I want to get involved' people crawling out of the fucking woodwork."

Most law enforcement officers hated it when an open case was aired on TV. Ninety-nine percent of the resulting callers had no real information pertaining to the case. You just had to be patient and weed through all of the false leads to get to the one that might solve the case. It was a tedious yet necessary process.

While the others headed off for their own assignments, Sean grabbed his laptop computer from his car and returned to the conference room they had used the day before. The sheriff had told the task force it was theirs for the duration of the case. The room had several dry-erase boards and corkboards on the walls, perfect for organizing victims, suspects, locations, and timelines. They were currently empty, but Sean planned to spend the day filling them with the data they had already gathered. It would help him identify any other similarities among the victims and develop a basic profile.

As he waited for the department's IT tech, who would interface his laptop with the department's system for easier access, his first order of business was to pin photos of the three victims onto one of the boards. In the top row, he placed pictures of the women as they had been in life—vibrant and alive. In the middle was a copy of their individual crime scene photos, and the bottom row contained photos of the victims in the autopsy suite. Next, he turned to one of the dry-erase boards and picked up a black marker sitting on the metal shelf beneath it.

He spent about an hour listing what they already knew about each victim and their crime scenes. By the time he finished that, his computer was ready to go. A department computer, fax machine, and printer had also been set up for the task force to use. As the technician left the room, Sean thanked him, then sat down at the conference table sin front of his laptop and signed himself into the FBI's National Data Exchange.

Most law enforcement agencies reported all major crimes in their jurisdictions to the FBI, whether or not they were solved. It wasn't mandatory nationwide, and some smaller police departments with low personnel numbers, crime rates, and financial budgets didn't have the resources to enter information into the system. But now, as more and more agencies moved forward into the computer era, very few major crimes escaped entry. The N-DEx database could be used to search for crimes with similar characteristics, such as DNA, weapons, or vehicles used, and modus operandi. Serial murderers, rapists, and other criminals tended to follow a pattern, or MO, when committing their crimes. The patterns might change slightly as the perpetrator honed his skills, but the basics tended to stay the same.

Once Sean entered the information they had gathered on the three murders into the program, the system would search for similar homicides throughout the United States. Young, blonde females, ligature strangulation, pennies, and "slut" carved into the torso—that was enough for a start. He set the program to compare those parameters against hundreds of thousands of cases in the database and spit out any that included at least three of the four catchphrases. Depending on how many cases were found, he would adjust the parameters.

It would take the program at least an hour to compile a list for him to start working on, so he moved to his next assignment, developing a basic profile of the UNSUB. Although Sean wasn't an FBI profiler, he had taken several courses on the subject provided by the bureau and had worked with a few of the FBI's criminal psychologists over the years.

He pulled out his phone to call Dr. Suki Ralston, his favorite shrink, who was stationed at the FBI head-quarters in Quantico, Virginia. He'd worked with her on three cases in the last two years and found her profiles of the suspects to be spot-on after they had been caught.

A Hawaiian native, Suki was a petite, dark-haired beauty with soft, caramel-colored skin who gave most men whiplash when she walked by. But while working on their first case together, Sean quickly found there was plenty more to the brilliant woman with a Ph.D. in criminal psychology than just her looks. She had a fun personality, a deep love of her career, and a wicked sense of humor.

After six weeks of long hours spent working together and then relaxing over several meals, the two had established a closeness similar to that of brother and sister. They'd kept in touch since their first case together, phoning each other a few times a month. He last spoke to Suki two weeks earlier, while he was packing to move back north, and had made tentative plans to meet her for dinner while he was still on vacation.

Finding her name in his list of cell phone contacts, he pressed send and waited for the call to go through. She picked it up on the third ring. "Hey, hot stuff, what's up?

Sean smiled at her teasing. "Aloha, Doc. How ya doing?"

"Great! How's your vacation going? Have you gone stir-crazy yet?"

"Actually, I'm working."

"What? You've got to be kidding me." After he told her he wasn't joking, she asked, "Didn't anyone teach you the definition of a vacation, Malone? You're what? Not even one week into a four-week stint? How the hell did you manage that?"

Sean took a moment to fill the profiler in on how he ended up with the case, then spent the next five minutes giving her the basic details of the murders. "That's it in a nutshell. So I called my favorite shrink to see if she could do a full profile for me. I've got just the basics."

"Favorite, huh? Well, flattery only gets you so far."

He laughed. "Uh-oh. What's it going to cost me this time? A king's ransom?"

"Nah. Just dinner, maybe dancing."

"Dinner, yes. Dancing—only if you don't mind getting your feet crushed. I'm a lousy dancer, or so my prom date told me way back when."

Suki giggled. "What? A stud-muffin like you doesn't have rhythm?"

His smile grew wider. "Oh, I've got rhythm, baby, just not on the dance floor."

The two chuckled with amusement. There was always innocent flirting going on between them, yet it'd never gone any further than that. Sean often wondered why he never asked her out. If Suki had been taller than her five-foot-three, she could have been a supermodel. He didn't deny the woman was gorgeous, but after working together, she quickly became a good friend, and he didn't want to ruin their relationship over a short fling. He knew it wouldn't last long—his relationships never did—and losing her friendship wasn't worth it to him. Besides, it was never a good thing to get involved with someone from the agency.

"Anyway," she said after she finally stopped laughing. "I've got a meeting in the morning at headquarters, but my afternoon is light and can be cleared. I'll fly down to you after the meeting, and you can show me what you have. I'll get a hotel room somewhere and start on the profile after you treat me to dinner. Sound good?"

"That'd be great, but you don't have to get a room. You can stay in the spare bedroom at my uncle's cottage."

"You don't have to put me up. I'll be fine in a hotel," she told him.

"I don't mind at all, and there's plenty of room. Besides, you haven't seen the place yet, and I know you love the beach. No more arguments."

"Okay, but if I get in your way, feel free to kick me out. Where should I meet you tomorrow?"

Sean gave her the Dare County Sheriff's Department address for her GPS. "Call me when you're almost here, and I'll meet you at the station."

"Perfect. Talk to you then."

After he disconnected the call, Deputy Montgomery walked into the room. "Got some good news for you, Agent Malone. Patrol found Stuart Crowell. Apparently, he ran after spotting them. Had some burglary tools with him. They got him, though. Should be pulling into the sally port just about now," he said, referring to the drive-in garage where prisoners were brought into the station, away from public view. The locked area also prevented suspects from trying to flee. "Detective Lynch is already on his way to booking—he asked for you to meet him there."

As Sean stood, the deputy handed him an electronic passkey. "The sheriff told me to give you this. It'll unlock most of the department doors without asking one of us to let you in."

He took the flat, plastic card and tucked it into his pants pocket. "That's great, thanks. How do I get to booking from here?"

"Far end of this hall, take the stairs down, make a right, and a quick left. You'll see the sign."

Before leaving the room, Sean left his computer program running but locked access to the laptop. Although it seemed silly since it was sitting in a police station, it was always better to be safe than sorry. One never knew who could be wandering around the halls —and they still didn't know who the leak was. There were also civilians working in various jobs in the department. He also locked the conference room door on his way out since the files were now spread out and information was on the boards.

He made his way through the station and walked into the booking area right behind Lynch. A sergeant and a booking deputy were already waiting for the prisoner when the sally port door opened. Two deputies entered, escorting a thin, white male wearing baggy clothes with his hands handcuffed behind his body. All three men were covered from head to toe in dark brown mud, and the two deputies looked ready to spit nails.

The sergeant took one look at the motley bunch and burst out laughing. "I can't wait to hear this one. What the hell happened?"

The two scowling deputies remained silent as they put the suspect in a holding cage and removed his handcuffs. The cage door was then slammed shut after they stepped back out.

The shorter and older of the two cocked his head toward the suspect. "We were driving around looking for this knucklehead and finally spotted him coming out of an alley off King Street. Took one look at us and ran toward the high school. We caught up with him on the football field, which, thanks to a broken sprinkler system, was a hundred yards of nothing but mud." The deputy looked at his partner's clothes, then at his own.

"Needless to say, Crowell here is also being charged with resisting arrest."

The other deputy snorted at his partner. "Johnson, man, I know you're not big on cursing, which in this job is unheard of, but at a time like this, feel free to call the guy a fucking asshole."

The rest of the men chuckled as the sergeant ordered, "You two go get cleaned up and into new uniforms before you do anything else. The detectives want to talk to him first anyway."

Crowell spoke up for the first time since walking into the station. "Hey, what about me? Don't I get to clean up too? I'm freezing. This is false arrest. I know my rights."

Both arresting deputies and the sergeant barked in unison, "Shut up!"

Johnson handed the booking deputy a plastic bag containing a wallet, a pack of cigarettes, and a few other items. "Here's his personal property. The rest of what we found on him will be logged into evidence."

"Hey, that's my stuff," Crowell whined. "You can't take my stuff. I have rights, you know."

Complaining suspects were always annoying, and at this point, everyone in booking yelled, "Shut up!" simultaneously.

The suspect mumbled to himself but wisely quieted down.

Chapter 6

Sean and Brad stood in an interrogation room as Stuart Crowell took a seat. The mud covering him was now dry and flaking all over the table, chair, and floor. Sean stifled a laugh as he watched the suspect try, unsuccessfully, to clean the dirt from under his fingernails. Under the circumstances, Crowell's actions were comical since nothing short of a waterfall would get the man clean. The two lawmen waited silently until the human mud pie finally looked up at them. "What?"

Neither man responded but continued to stare until the suspect started to squirm under the dark scrutiny. Lynch finally moved from where he'd been leaning against a wall to stand opposite Crowell. "Where were you this past Saturday night and Sunday morning?"

The suspect shrugged his shoulders as if he were bored. "I don't know."

Lynch leaned forward and slammed his hands on the table, causing Crowell to jump back, almost falling off the chair. "You'd better know," the detective growled in a low voice. "Cause I've got a dead body that you're looking good for."

"Wh... what?" Crowell's eyes became as wide as saucers. He began to panic, rapidly looking back and forth between the two men. "I didn't kill no one! No fucking way, man! You got the wrong guy! I never killed anyone!"

"Well, then, help us clear you," Sean said in a sympathetic tone of voice. He took the role of good cop to the detective's bad cop. "Tell us where you were Saturday and Sunday."

"I... I don't remember."

Lynch smacked the table again.

Crowell flinched. "Wait a minute. Wait a minute. Um, Sunday... Sunday, I was working most of the day. Yeah, that's where I was." A look of relief came over his face as he realized he had an alibi.

"Working where?"

"The Auto Zone in the Caldwell Shopping Center. I was there from ten in the morning 'til five."

Leaning on his hands, Lynch scowled at the suspect. "What about the rest of the day and late Saturday night between eleven and one thirty?"

"Before and after work, I was home. My mom can

vouch for me. She saw me. And Saturday... um... where was I?" Crowell tapped the table with his fingers in frustration before his face lit up. "Oh yeah!"

His relieved expression immediately fell. "Uh-oh."

"Uh-oh?" Lynch raised his eyebrows. "What the fuck does uh-oh mean?"

"If I tell you, I'm screwed."

The detective raised his voice again. "And if you don't tell us, you're screwed. Now, where the fuck were you?"

"Shit, man, this is so messed up," the suspect mumbled, his eyes downcast. "I was... I was over in Wanchese with a buddy of mine."

"And?"

The reason for Crowell's reluctance to talk suddenly became clear to Sean. "And you were burglarizing someone's house, weren't you?"

Crowell nodded reluctantly. Because the suspect had just admitted to committing a crime, the interview became an official interrogation, and Lynch read him his Miranda rights. "Do you understand these rights?"

The suspect rolled his eyes. "Yeah. I've fucking heard them before."

"Are you willing to speak to us without your lawyer?"

"Whatever. If I don't, you'll pin the murder on me."

Sliding a Miranda waiver across the table for Crowell to sign, Brad tossed a pen on top of it and waited until the signature was in its proper place. "What's the address of the house you hit?"

The thief glanced up at him with a defeated look on his face. "I don't remember the number, but it was on Pond Road. White with red trim."

Lynch left the pen on the table and replaced the waiver with a yellow legal pad. "Write down every-thing you took. If it matches the police report of what the homeowner said was taken and when the burglary occurred, we can probably clear you of the homicide."

"But now I'm on the hook for the burglary, right?"

"Five to seven is better than twenty-five to life."

Crowell sighed and picked up the pen again.

At ten after five, Sheriff Griffin and the task force members sat in the conference room with frustrated expressions. After bringing Stuart Crowell back to the booking cell, Sean and Lynch went out to substantiate his alibi. His boss verified that Stuart had been there from ten to five on Sunday, and his mother said he was home before and after work. Two of his neighbors also confirmed they saw Crowell's car in his driveway when he was supposedly home, and they didn't see him leave in another car or on foot.

Lynch pulled the burglary report from 31 Pond Road, and the stolen inventory matched Crowell's list of what he and his buddy had taken from the residence. The only issue they still had was Crowell refused to say who his partner in crime had been. But all the evidence cleared him for Daphne Jones's homicide, so Sean didn't care if the guy wanted to take full responsibility for the burglary. The case had been transferred to the property crimes detectives—it was their problem now.

Brian and Rafe reported they'd had little success with their interviews. While several of the nightclub's employees remembered seeing Daphne in her tight, red dress, no one recalled seeing her with anyone in particular, and they didn't see her leave the bar.

Lynch stated he had no luck with the surveillance tape from the club. While Daphne was spotted several times, he couldn't get a clear picture of anyone she was talking to or dancing with. "The vic must have left through the back door of the place because I didn't see her on the front door video. Unfortunately, the video for the back is worse than the rest. It was too fucking distorted to distinguish anyone, and since it was in black and white, I couldn't even look for a red dress."

"Did our UNSUB know the video equipment sucked, tamper with it himself, or did he just get lucky?" Sean wondered aloud as he leaned back in his chair.

Brad rubbed his tired, dry eyes. "Lucky would be my guess. For a popular place, they have a shit surveillance setup. It looks like the lenses are dirty from smoke and grime. Probably haven't been cleaned since they were installed. There's no sign of tampering with the cameras or digital system. So we're back at square one—no suspects and no leads."

"And no idea who his next victim is," Brian added wryly.

"Shit." The detective's gaze zipped to Sean's. "Anything on similar homicides in N-DEx?"

He shook his head. "No. There's a glitch in the system, and the program's temporarily down—what else is fucking new? The HQ techs are working on it, and I'm told they should have it running again in the morning. As soon as it's up, I'll re-enter the parameters."

Lynch let out an exasperated breath. "Jeez, can't catch a fucking break today, can we? Does anyone have anything positive to add to this mess?"

Sean stood and stretched his shoulders and neck. He pushed an image of Grace giving him a massage from his mind. "Well, I've got one of the best FBI profilers coming to see us tomorrow afternoon. Her name's Suki Ralston. I've worked with her on a few cases, and the woman knows her stuff."

"I know you feds claim profiling has helped in the past, but does it really work, or is it just a fucking guessing game? I mean—"

Griffin held up his hand, cutting the other man off mid-sentence. "It could be fucking voodoo for all I care, but if it helps us catch this bastard, I'm all for it."

Looking up at Sean, he asked, "What time is she coming?"

"She's flying into Elizabeth City from Quantico and should be here sometime after two. Knowing her, she'll dig right in and be up half the night going through the files. My guess is she'll have a preliminary profile ready first thing Thursday morning." He turned to Brad. "And the answer to your question is *yes*, it does work, but it won't hand you your suspect on a silver platter like the general public seems to think, although I wish it did. It's just another tool to use to narrow down your search."

The sheriff stood and started for the door. "Sounds good. Lynch, update your file and leave a copy on my desk. Everyone else, I'll see you in the morning." He paused at the doorway. "Oh, and I'd like all of you to be with me at tomorrow's press conference at eleven. The commissioner and mayor want the public to see we're using every available resource to solve this. You don't have to be at every one of them. Maybe every few days until this is over. Politics, politics, gotta love fucking politics."

Brad grabbed his file and headed for the door. "Smile pretty for the cameras, boys."

The other men groaned. Dealing with the press and politicians was always a pain in the ass for law enforcement, but sometimes they were a necessary evil. If you kissed their asses often enough, they might help out somehow when you really needed it.

Montoya and the Malone brothers said goodnight to the chief and detective and walked out to the station's parking lot. Montoya gave the others a quick goodbye before hopping into his car and driving off. He'd mentioned earlier his nephew's high school baseball team was playing its first game of the season against their biggest rival, and if Rafe hurried, he could catch the end of it.

Brian's navy blue Dodge Ram was parked two spaces away from Sean's Mustang. When they reached their vehicles, Sean looked at his brother. "I'm starving. What do you say to dinner and a few beers at Sassy's?"

The local restaurant was a few doors down from their uncle's hardware store and had been a favorite among Whisper's residents for many years. Before Bonnie had taught Dan how to cook nutritious meals for his three orphaned nephews, the Malone teenagers and their uncle had spent many nights eating at Sassy's. The restaurant's namesake had passed away several years ago, but her daughter and son-in-law had taken over the business and kept it thriving.

Tossing his keys in the air, Brian caught them again. "Sorry, bro. I get together with some guys from work on Thursday evenings for a little three-on-three basketball at the 'Y.' We usually go out afterward for a few beers, though. Why don't you come with us?"

"No, thanks. I just want to sit and relax tonight, maybe catch a game on TV. You go ahead, and I'll see you in the morning."

"You sure?"

Sean nodded. "Yeah. I'll just stop, pick up a six-pack, and chill on the couch."

"All right. See you tomorrow."

"Later."

* * *

Grace steered her shopping cart up and down the aisles of the Stop and Go grocery store. Two blocks away from her PT office, the store wasn't as large as most chain supermarkets, yet it still had plenty of name brands, a full buffet of hot food for when you weren't in the mood to cook, and a wide variety of fresh coffee beans to choose from.

As she strolled through the aisles, her thoughts turned to Sean. This was nothing new since she had been thinking of him all day. She'd really had a fun time the evening before, and all they had done was sit on the floor and share a pizza. He'd walked into Pro-Care wearing a sports coat over a T-shirt and jeans, which fit him like a glove. He'd looked yummy with the coat on, but when he took it off, and she saw the snug fit of the tee over his sculpted chest and shoul-ders—Lord, help her, he'd been downright gorgeous. His body was hard and tight. Her hands had ached to touch his shoulders, chest, arms, and back and feel every contour. A lock of his hair had kept falling down over his forehead, and she wished she'd been courageous enough to reach out and stroke it back into place.

She sighed. Oh, well, back to reality.

Aside from daydreaming about the sexy Sean Malone, it had been a long yet productive day, and although she was hungry, she wasn't in the mood to fix a big dinner. She'd just picked up a hot, precooked chicken to place in her basket when she heard a *tsk tsk* behind her. Spinning around, she found herself looking into a pair of teasing, mocha-brown eyes, and her heart skipped a beat. She'd been thinking of the man all day —hell, she'd been thinking of him just a few seconds ago—and now here he was, standing in front of her, grinning that adorable grin that made her insides flutter.

"What?" she asked as a smile spread across her face.

"Bonnie would have a fit if she saw you buying any pre-made food."

Grace laughed. "Only if it's frozen and processed. A fresh chicken is okay in her book. Besides, I already grabbed the fixings for a salad and a baked potato to go with it."

Sean rubbed his growling stomach. "Stop! You're making me even hungrier. And to tell you the truth, I'm getting one of those chickens for my own dinner, along with a beer or two."

"Why should we get two chickens when we can

split one?" Grace queried, hoping he would agree. "I'll get the food, you grab the beer."

"Sounds good to me." He raised his eyebrows and lowered his voice, so it was dramatically sexy. "So, babe, your place or mine?"

She laughed at his antics. "Um, mine, if it doesn't matter to you. I have a few things in here that need to be refrigerated." She indicated her half-full cart. "Besides, you haven't seen my new place yet."

"All right then. You grab another potato, I'll get us a six-pack, and we'll meet at the checkout line." He turned, then glanced back over his shoulder. "You know, this is the first time I've ever picked up a woman in a grocery store."

Chapter 7

s Grace tossed the salad, Sean poured two bottles of beer into a pair of pilsner glasses from her kitchen cabinet. He'd already set the table, and they were waiting for the potatoes to finish cooking in the microwave. They both agreed it wasn't the best way to cook potatoes, but since everything else was ready, faster was better in this situation. She checked the timer on the potatoes and then opened the bottom broiler of the oven to see if the garlic bread was ready.

"This is a great kitchen," Sean stated from behind her, taking a moment to enjoy the view of her shapely ass as she bent over. "There's plenty of room for two people to work without tripping over each other." He didn't mention how comfortable he felt with her as they moved about the room preparing their meal. They worked well together as if they had been doing it for years.

After sliding the toasted bread out onto a cutting board, she closed the broiler door and stood. "That's one of the reasons I picked this place. All the rooms are a nice size, there's plenty of closet space, and it's an end unit, so I have extra windows."

Sean sipped his beer and peeked through the kitchen doorway into the living room. "I see you haven't done much decorating yet unless cardboard boxes are the 'in' thing now."

Grace giggled as she set the salad bowl on the kitchen table. "Not that I know of, but if it is, then I'm good. I just haven't had much time to unpack yet. I want Pro-Care up and running first, then I can work on this place."

"Good. And when you're done here, you can help me decorate my apartment. Everything is in storage while they paint and replace the old cabinetry and carpeting, but after I move in, my décor will be brown, cardboard boxes, too."

Her laugh was infectious. "It's nice to know we have the same decorating style. Have a seat—every-thing's ready."

Grabbing the plate with the potatoes from the microwave, he sat in the chair she'd indicated but waited until she joined him before putting food on his plate. "Nice to know we have the same culinary apti-tude too."

"Two peas in a pod." She handed him a basket filled with garlic bread slices and a bowl of cranberry jelly. Sitting down across the small table from him, she began to fill her own plate with food.

Putting a slab of butter on his potato, he grinned at the domesticity of their meal. "So, honey, how was your day at work? Anything exciting happen?"

Grace chuckled at his teasing. It did almost feel like they were a couple having a routine dinner together. She played along. "Well, dear. I was very busy. I spent the morning doctor shopping, introducing myself, and trying to drum up some patient referrals. I hit as many as I could from the north end of Dare County. Over the next few days, I'll do the south end and a few in Elizabeth City. The physicians I saw today were happy to hear I was opening since there are so few PT clinics in the area outside of the hospitals."

"That's good." Sean finished preparing his plate and set it on the table before picking up his fork and knife. "Very little competition. What else did you do, Mrs. Cleaver?"

"Mrs. Cleaver, huh? Since when did you get old enough to have watched *Leave It To Beaver*?"

"Hey, at least you got the reference. Unless you're older than fifty these days, that one goes over most people's heads."

She grinned. "Very true. Let's see. I went to Staples to pick out a few filing cabinets, clipboards, pens, paper, folders, and everything else I'll need in the office. It's amazing how fast you can burn through a thousand dollars in that store."

"Holy shit," Sean retorted, almost choking on a piece of chicken. "No wonder the supply clerks are always bitching at work when I need office stuff."

"Yup," she replied. "Anyway, after that, I finished painting the silhouettes. Tomorrow I'm interviewing the PT applicants. Then all I need is the furniture and equipment to be delivered, and I'll be ready to open. Oh, and I have to go to Best Buy and get a flat-screen TV for the patients to watch if they want. There tends to be a lot of lying around when you're in PT."

Sean had a brief mental picture of Brian lying on one of the PT tables as Grace gave him a back massage. He quickly shook the image from his mind. Only when hell froze over if he had anything to say about it. It took a moment to realize Grace was talking again, and he tried to focus on what she was saying.

"...on the radio about the three women who were murdered. That's the case you're working on, isn't it?"

He grimaced and nodded. "Yeah, what a mess, too."

"Want to talk about it? I mean, what you can talk about."

Sean shrugged. He could at least tell her what had already been released to the press, maybe a little bit more. He just couldn't tell her about the pennies or carvings, not that he would bring those up at the dinner table anyway. "Three women in three months

—all between the ages of twenty-two and thirty-two. All taken from public areas after partying somewhere. Strangled then dumped in public places—although the last one was a little more concealed than the first two... you sure you want to hear this over dinner?"

Grace let out a small sigh. "It is kind of morbid table talk, isn't it? So, what else have you been doing since you moved back?"

They finished dinner while discussing the changes they'd both noted around Whisper and several places from their youth that were now gone. After they put their plates in the dishwasher, Sean poured them each another beer, and they moved to the living room. Since the only thing not covered with boxes was the couch, they sat down at either end. Sean wanted to move a little closer, so he could smell Grace's perfume, which had been driving him crazy all evening with a whiff here and there, but he didn't trust himself not to try and kiss her.

They sat and chatted for a long time about anything that came to mind before Grace let out a sudden yawn. "I'm sorry," she apologized. "It's not the company. It's just been a long day."

Sean glanced at his watch and found it was later than he thought. "Yeah. I'd better get going, or we'll both be dragging our asses in the morning."

Grace stood with him and walked him to the door.

"Thanks for dinner," he said, turning back to her.

She giggled. "I'm glad you liked it after I slaved over a hot stove all day to make it."

He chuckled and leaned forward to kiss her on the cheek, but Grace moved her head at the last moment, and their lips touched. He froze in shock for a second, then his body took over, and he deepened the kiss. She was so sweet, he didn't think he would ever forget her taste. And he wanted more.

As her arms went around his neck, he put his hands on her waist and pulled her closer. The moment her soft breasts touched his rock-hard chest, Grace jumped back as if struck by a jolt of electricity. They were both breathless, staring at each other with expressions of desire mingled with confusion.

"Um... wow. I... um," Sean stuttered, then cleared his throat. "I'd better get going before I do something crazy like take you to bed."

"Yeah," Grace agreed, swallowing hard as she tried to slow her breathing. "That would be crazy... just—"

"Crazy," he finished for her, his voice low and husky as his eyes focused on her lush lips. With tremendous difficulty, he managed to convince himself he had to leave. As much as he did want to throw her onto a bed and fuck her silly, he knew it would be best to take things slowly. Tracing a finger along her jawline, he whispered, "Goodnight, Grace."

Satisfaction coursed through him when she shivered. "Goodnight, Sean."

* * *

"... and the Sheriff's Department is not releasing any more information about the homicides at this time, but we will continue to keep the public updated. This is Jessica Daly for the Channel Four evening news."

George Wallace hummed a silly tune to himself as the screen returned to the male news anchor, who moved on to some inconsequential story. So, he'd made the news. This was the first time, and he felt empowered and high about the publicity. It was about time his work was acknowledged, and soon people would figure out it was for the best. He was ridding the world of worthless women. Grinning, he went back to his dinner, thinking of future possibilities. Life was good—at least for him.

* * *

The next morning, Sean sat in the conference room trying to concentrate on the N-DEx program on his laptop, but his mind kept wandering to Grace and the kiss they'd shared—brief as it was. He'd been so wound up when he got home that he took care of his hard-on in the shower before climbing into bed. And yet his dreams of her had forced him to take a cold one several hours later when he awakened before sunrise.

It was obvious they'd both enjoyed the kiss—the flames in her eyes had told him she'd been as affected by it as he had. But now, he couldn't help but think taking things further might ruin a longtime friendship. It had been years since he'd last seen Grace, but there was still a closeness between them. Yet, what did he really know about her? Fourteen years and transitioning from child to adult made a big difference in a person. And what would Bonnie and Uncle Dan say? Would they be happy about a budding romance between the two, or would they discourage it?

He was so engrossed in his thoughts he never heard his brother and Rafe enter the room. Brian crept up behind him and flicked his left ear, causing Sean to jump from his chair and whirl around, ready to fight. "Fuck you, asshole. Haven't you learned yet not to do that to someone carrying a gun?"

His brother let out a deep belly laugh. "Been doing that to you since we were little, and I still get away with it. You make it too easy being in la-la land. What were you thinking about?"

If Brian only knew where Sean's mind had been, he would be teasing him all day. "Nothing really," he lied, taking his seat again. "Just trying to wrap my head around this serial."

"What time is your profiler getting here?" Montoya asked. "I've never had the opportunity to work with one before, and I'm actually looking forward to it. Should be interesting after all the reading I've done on the subject.

"Around two, I think. Suki's gonna call from the road when she gets closer."

Rafe's eyebrows shot up. "Suki? Interesting name. Asian?"

"She's originally from Hawaii, but I think she once told me there was Korean in her family background. Oh, and do me a favor, guys, don't fucking hit on her."

"*Ah*, she's hot then," Brian stated with a smile.

Sighing, he shook his head. "Yes, she's good-looking, but she's also a good friend of mine and a respected federal agent with a doctorate, so show her some fucking respect while she's here. Okay, asshole?"

"If you insist." Despite his assent, Brian sat across the table from Sean with a silly leer on his face. He loved busting his younger brother's chops.

Sean threw a pen at his sibling and then pulled his laptop closer. It was time to stop fucking around and catch themselves a killer. While the two state agents added the information they'd learned yesterday to the whiteboards, Sean began to enter the case parameters back into the program, which was once again up and running. Hopefully, in an hour or so, they'd have a potential lead or two from the system.

After a daily morning briefing with the detective bureau's lieutenant, Brad Lynch joined the rest of the task force. The men began throwing out ideas and theories, yet they were frustrated by how little they had to go on. It seemed like criminals were getting smarter every year, with shows like CSI and NCIS on television and websites all over the internet that demonstrated how to commit a crime and get away with it.

Just as the group was running out of ideas, Sean's computer sounded an alert. It'd found a connection to his parameters. He quickly printed out the information and relayed it to the others. "We got a hit—a good match too. Last year in Philadelphia. Three female victims over a three-month period—July through September. All blondes in their twenties. Taken after partying somewhere. Found at least twenty-four hours later in public locations." Looking up at the rest of the task force, he added with a combination of disgust and excitement, "And all had pennies left on their foreheads and 'slut' carved into their torsos."

Brad's eyes went wide. "Shit! I don't remember hearing anything about that, and it's not like Pennsylvania's on the other side of the fucking country. Didn't it make the news?"

"I don't know, but there's an FBI case file open on it. No viable suspects, though. I'll call the lead agent up there—see if I can get my hands on the file and whatever info he's got. Or *she's* got," he amended, glancing at the bottom of the page he held. "Says here, Agent Karen Winslow, out of the local office there. Why don't one of you call Philly PD and try to find out what they have on it?"

Montoya pulled out his cell phone. "I'll do it. I've got a few contacts up there."

"Sounds good," Lynch said. "The rest of us will

continue digging into the victims' pasts. See if we can find out how he's choosing his vics." He paused a moment, thinking over the information they'd just received. "You know, we might also have another problem on our hands. Is he killing three, then moving on? Is he done here? Or are we just dicking around until he kills another one?"

Those were hard questions to answer. On one hand, they hoped there were no more murders in their jurisdiction, but on the other, they wanted this bastard. If killing three victims and moving on was part of the killer's pattern, he may have already left North Carolina for God-only-knew-where.

Sheriff Griffin stepped into the room and asked for an update. After they filled him in on the Pennsylvania connection, he crossed his arms and leaned against the wall next to the door. "All right. Let's keep this quiet for now. I want everyone at this morning's press conference at eleven, unless something urgent comes up. We'll give the fucking sharks the same info we gave them yesterday, just spin it differently so it sounds new. I asked the medical examiner to attend, but he won't release much info either. As you know, the press already found out the first two victims' names, somehow. I spoke to Daphne Jones's father in Chicago around six last night after the local PD broke the news to the family, so we can also release her name. Everyone, meet in my office at ten of eleven, and we'll walk out together."

Without waiting for any responses, the tired-looking leader returned to his office.

Sean looked at Lynch. "Where do you hold your press conferences?"

"In the lobby on bad days," the man answered. "But the weather's nice today, so it'll probably be on the front steps of the station. Anyway, we have two hours until then, so let's get to work."

The two NCSP detectives left to re-interview the victims' families and friends, while Lynch headed back to his desk in the detective bureau to work through the new batch of hotline messages. Sean picked up one of several phones on the conference table and dialed the number for Agent Karen Winslow, which was listed on the report in front of him.

He was surprised and pleased when she answered on the second ring. "Special Agent Winslow."

"Agent Winslow, this is Agent Sean Malone in Elizabeth City, North Carolina."

"What can I do for you, Agent Malone?"

He grabbed a nearby legal pad and a pen. "Sean, please."

"Then feel free to call me Karen. Now that we have the niceties out of the way, what can I help you with?"

Sean got straight to the point. "Well, it seems we have a serial down here who matches one you had last year in Philly. Pennies on the forehead and the word 'slut' carved into the vics' torsos."

He could almost hear the female agent sit up straighter on the other end of the line. "Holy shit! How many has he killed down there?"

He sighed. "Three in the past three months."

"Fuck! Goddamn this bastard."

"How did your homicides stay out of the news up there? I never heard about them until I got the hit in N-DEx."

"We got lucky," Winslow admitted. "The first one was a prostitute—no one claimed the body, so she was sent to a potter's grave. Must have been a busy news day, and without details of how she died, the press wasn't interested. The second one was, and still is, a Jane Doe. We think she may have been a transient, passing through the area, but we couldn't match her to any missing persons, and got no leads after running a police sketch on the news. We didn't release the fact she was a homicide victim—just an unattended death. She spent four months at the morgue before being buried next to the first vic.

"The third one was new to the area. After the body was released, the family brought her back home to Vermont. Anyway, no one except the local detectives and us knew about their connection. And I think for the first time in my career, there were no leaks from the PD or medical examiner's office."

"You're right," Sean agreed. "You got damn lucky. I was hoping you could share what you have in your files."

"I can overnight everything to you." He heard her shuffling papers around. "Give me a phone number where I can reach you and your email so I can send you some preliminary stuff. Then the address for the file." Sean gave her all the information she'd requested before she added, "I wish I could come down there and assist you. Unfortunately, I have to appear in court this week. Damn, I want this fucking bastard bad."

"You and me both. We also have a profiler driving in from Quantico."

"Who's coming?"

He leaned back in his chair. "Doctor Suki Ralston. Do you know her?"

"Absolutely! I've worked with Suki on several cases. Was hoping to get her last year for this one, but she was unavailable. Listen, I have to run—I just sent you an email containing the initial reports and autopsy results. I'll overnight the copies of the rest. Let me know if you have any questions or leads."

"No problem. Wait, one more thing. What were the dates on the pennies? Were they all the same?"

"Yeah. They were all from 1993. Yours?"

"Same here, 1993. Another unknown piece to the puzzle. All right, I'll let you know if we find anything, and thanks." When Sean hung up, he received the new email on his laptop. Sending the documents to the printer, he hoped there was something in there to give them a lead or two before this psycho killed again.

Chapter 8

By a quarter to eleven, Sean was more frustrated than ever. The information in the Philadelphia files brought him no closer to understanding the killer. The women from Pennsylvania could have been carbon copies of the ones from North Carolina in the looks department—blonde, in their twenties, with similar body types. The pennies, carvings, and public dump scenes also tied them all together. But that's where the differences ended.

The three local vics had all been working women—in legal professions—while only the last one in Philly had worked and gone missing from a nightclub. The first one had probably been picked up by the suspect posing as a john, and investigators had never figured out where victim number two had encountered her killer.

Sean now had three new victims to add to the time-line, but the suspect count still stood at zero. "Fuck."

Sean stood and stretched as Brad, Brian, and Rafe entered the room. They looked as frustrated as he felt. Since they were due in Sheriff Griffin's office in a few minutes, the group decided to wait until after the press conference to compare notes.

Griffin met them in the hallway. "Let's get this over with. God, I fucking hate these things."

The sheriff had donned his formal dress uniform for the press meeting. Sean and the others were all wearing two-piece suits, white dress shirts, and subdued ties—very professional. The somber group started down the hall toward the lobby.

"By the way," Griffin said, "the ME can't make it. His mother broke her hip this morning, and he's at the hospital with her. Sean, the press will want to hear from the FBI, so be prepared for some questions."

"No problem."

As Lynch had told them earlier, the department's press liaison, Sergeant Zweig, and Captain Dworski had set up the conference on the front steps of the station. On the top step stood a wooden lectern with over a dozen microphones. Griffin approached it and spent the next five minutes updating the crowd of tele-vision and print reporters scattered on the steps and walkway. He released Daphne Jones's name as the sergeant handed out copies of the photo of her that her roommate had given them. The picture had been taken with Cheryl Armstrong's iPhone the night she'd gone missing, and it showed Daphne's smiling face, full of life. A life that was snuffed out a few hours later.

The sheriff asked for anyone who may have seen Daphne at Visions the night she was abducted to contact the task force and provided the department's special phone number for information. He also said they would accept any tips about the other victims.

Sean was a little shocked at how many reporters there were. Apparently, when the local broadcast of a serial killer in Dare County hit the news, it had attracted an even larger audience, twice as many reporters as the day before. There were news vans from all over the state, as well as a few from across the Virginia border, Washington, D.C., and even one from CNN. By this evening, the task force would be on national television from coast to coast. Most killers loved the attention they garnered from their crimes, and Sean hated contributing to that, but it was a necessary evil. They would need the public's help to solve these murders or a whole lot of luck. He didn't care how they caught the killer—as long as they did.

"I'd like to introduce the members of the task force," Griffin said into the multitude of microphones perched on the lectern he stood behind. "Lead detective, Brad Lynch, of the Dare County Sheriff's Department. Detectives Rafe Montoya and Brian Malone of the SBI. And Special Agent Sean Malone of the

Greenville FBI office." He turned to Sean. "Agent Malone, would you like to make a statement?"

Not really. "Yes, Sheriff Griffin. Thank you." He replaced the sheriff in the hot seat. Basically, he repeated what Griffin had already told them, adding that the FBI was doing everything it could to assist the local law enforcement agencies.

"Agent Malone," one male reporter yelled out. "Are there any suspects yet? And if not, has the FBI developed a profile of the killer yet?

"As Sheriff Griffin already stated, there are no official suspects yet, but we have several leads and are looking for anyone who may have known or come across any of the three victims at one time or another. As for your second question, we expect an FBI profiler to arrive this afternoon from Quantico to assist us."

"Agent Malone, are you new to the FBI?" This came from a busty, bleached-blonde female reporter on the other side of the crowd. Sean was surprised at the question, and before he had a chance to recover, the woman added, "I tried to contact you through the Greenville office yesterday and was told you hadn't officially started working there yet. Are you from another office? Is there a connection to other homicides in another state?"

Sean shot a glance at Griffin. The woman was hitting a little too close to home for his comfort. Where the hell was she getting her information from? "No, I'm not new to the FBI. I've been assigned to the

Jacksonville, Florida, office for over seven years. I'm originally from North Carolina and recently transferred back here for family reasons." He deliberately didn't mention the homicides in Pennsylvania. The longer they kept a lid on the cases up there, the better.

Sheriff Griffin wisely stepped back to the lectern at that moment and ended the press conference. "We'll hold another press conference at the same time tomorrow. But for now, there's nothing else we're releasing to the public. Please remind your female viewers to take extra precautions and not go out alone. They should travel in pairs and groups, avoid being alone around strangers, lock their doors, and be extra vigilant. If any member of the public has any information pertaining to this case, they can call our tip line. Thank you, ladies and gentlemen."

Several reporters shouted more questions, but the lawmen ignored them, returning to privacy behind the electronically locked door inside the station.

When they were finally away from the microphones, Sean repeated his earlier thought aloud. "Where the hell are they getting their information, and how the fuck did that reporter get my name? Does anyone know who she is and who she works for?"

"Jessica Daly, Channel Four News in Greenville, but she covers Dare and Currituck Counties," Brad told him as they entered their conference room. "And she's a bitch, a shark, and a mongrel with a bone all rolled into one. Always seems to be one step ahead of the other local stations.

"I've been on the receiving end of one of her quote-unquote investigations. She tried hitting on me to get information. I wouldn't touch her with a ten-foot pole. She may be hot, but she's too ambitious for her own good. Even if I wasn't happily married, she's definitely not my type.

"Be careful around that one. She's gonna get herself into trouble one of these days. I'd love to know where she's getting her info, though."

Sean shed his jacket and hung it on the back of a chair. "So would I."

They all took seats at the oblong table and began to update each other and the sheriff with what they had learned since the morning briefing. Sean handed out copies of the reports Agent Winslow had emailed him. "She's overnighting the rest of the stuff."

Lynch took his copy of the reports and glanced at them. "Hey, what time does your profiler get in? My wife's friend is the manager of the Days Inn up the street. I can call her and have a room set up for your agent. How many nights will she be here?"

"I haven't a clue. But it's... uh... no problem," Sean replied. "I offered her the spare bedroom at the beach house."

"Oh, really?" his brother teased. "Getting cozy with the doc, huh? What happened to little Gracie?"

The younger Malone rolled his eyes. "As I said

before, asshole, Suki's a friend—nothing more. I told her to take one of the spare bedrooms because it's nicer than staying in a motel."

Sean didn't mention Grace, but now he realized she might take Suki staying at the cottage the wrong way. He'd have to introduce them to each other and explain to Grace that he had no romantic interest in Suki.

Why did it feel like he just dug himself into a deep hole?

* * *

Grace sighed with relief as the last physical therapist she'd interviewed left Pro-Care a few minutes after noon. Up until applicant number four, she'd thought she would never find another PT for the business. She wondered how numbers one through three had even graduated high school, much less gotten their physical therapy certifications. However, Tim Koppel, applicant number four, was perfect for the job. He was intelligent, friendly, seemed to have good references, and knew his stuff.

The forty-eight-year-old was a widower and father of two teenage boys. He'd been a physical therapist for almost twenty years in Seattle and had moved his boys to North Carolina to be closer to the rest of his family after his wife died of cancer two years earlier. He was currently working at one of the hospitals in Currituck

County but heard he might be losing his job soon due to cutbacks and layoffs. Deciding not to wait for that to happen, he'd applied for the job with Grace as soon as he'd heard about it.

When she explained it was a new business and might be slow as they worked to develop a clientele, he responded he had no problem with that. Koppel had confided in her that he had an eye for investments and made enough money in the stock market to retire, but he was afraid he would be bored to tears if he did. Besides that, he loved working with people.

Grace would double-check his references this afternoon, and if all went well, she'd call him in the morning to offer him the job.

Now that she had staff and a place, she just needed the equipment to be delivered, and she was good to go. She wanted to call Sean with the good news but didn't want to disturb him at work. Maybe she'd stop by the beach house later to see him. In the meantime, she needed to go purchase the television and stop at the sign company to see the Pro-Care sign, which would be mounted outside her business above the door and picture window. They wanted her approval before delivering and installing it.

She was just grabbing her coat and purse when there was a strange scratching noise coming from the front door. Laughter burst from her when she saw Dan Malone's dog, Jinx, sitting on the other side of the glass, "knocking" at her door with his paw. He had an adorable face and a piece of paper in his mouth.

She unlocked the door and opened it. Jinx's tail wagged in earnest when she squatted down to his level and gave his ears a good scratching before taking the paper from him. Unfolding it, she read aloud, *"Come join us for lunch at Dan's. Love, Aunt Bonnie."*

She grinned at Jinx. "I guess this is a formal invitation, huh, boy?"

The dog woofed his response, causing Grace to start laughing again. "You won't take no for an answer, will you?"

Jinx shook himself from nose to tail, turned, and, after looking both ways as his human counterparts would, trotted back across the street to the hardware store.

Grace hadn't realized how hungry she was until now, so she decided to join the older couple for a bite to eat. She knew Bonnie occasionally closed her shop for a half hour during lunch while leaving a sign in her boutique window saying she could be reached at the hardware store in an emergency.

She often wondered why Dan and her aunt never became romantically involved. As far as Grace knew, Bonnie hadn't dated in years, and Dan had never remarried after losing his wife to cancer while they were both still in their twenties. Thirty-five years was a long time to live without someone special to love.

Anyway, lunch first, errands second.

* * *

George Wallace sat at the lunch counter of a local greasy spoon he frequented, waiting for his sandwich and watching the end of the twelve o'clock newscast with interest.

I've made the news again, he thought with pride and decided to record the evening news later to save as a memento. He hadn't stayed in Pennsylvania long enough to garner any press up there, but apparently, he was big news here in North Carolina. He was now convinced moving to the house he'd inherited from his deceased aunt had been a great idea. The warmer weather would also bring tourists and beach bunnies who loved to show off their slutty, little bodies in two-piece bathing suits. Just thinking of potential victims made his mouth water.

"Here ya go." He was snapped out of his fantasies by the waitress putting his lunch before him. "Can I get you anything else, George?"

"No thanks, Anita—this looks perfect."

Anita smiled. "Well, enjoy. Let me know if you need anything."

"I will." He picked up half of the huge BLT and took a big bite.

He liked Anita. An older, plump brunette with hints of gray, she was never anything but happy and kind. He often wished she were his mother.

At a very young age, George learned to fend for

himself. He'd loved school and went every day, holding an A minus/B plus average throughout his sixteen years of public education. It gave him a reprieve from his shitty home life that had included his mother's drinking binges, scream fests, and beatings, which usually occurred in that order.

His mother had been a lazy-assed, bleached-blonde bimbo who sent him off to the movies every weekend so she could entertain her johns to subsidize what she received from the state in welfare and food stamps— the government wouldn't pay for all the alcohol she liked to drink. He'd only been a little kid, and she'd told him to walk three blocks to the theater, by himself, with a handful of loose change. He had to buy a movie ticket with a bunch of quarters, nickels, dimes, and pennies, while she was charging men a lot more than that to do disgusting things with them.

What kind of mother did that? A lousy, worthless one.

He'd needed to save the change the whore gave him for a few days, sometimes over a week, to have enough money for a movie to get away from his miserable life. In the meantime, he'd go to the zoo on free Wednesdays or the park. Even though it hadn't cost anything to get into the zoo, he still had to sneak in since the attendants usually questioned his age and wanted to know where his parent or guardian was.

He could still remember the look on one woman's face when he'd responded, "Fucking some guy for money." Guess she hadn't expected a seven-year-old to say something like that.

But little did Wanda Wallace know, as her son got older, he'd kept the paltry bit of change she gave him but didn't leave the house when instructed. Instead, he watched her and her clients from a small hole he'd drilled into the back of the closet in his room, which was next to his mother's bedroom. The more he watched the fucking slut in action, the more he hated her, which worked out well because she hated him. His mother had constantly reminded him of how she got stuck with him after his good-for-nothing father took off as soon as she'd told him she was pregnant.

He never did get into the zoo that day since he'd run after the attendant had wanted to call the police to help him. They wouldn't help him—they never did. Usually, they just stuck him in horrible foster homes whenever his mother was in jail, then returned him to her after she promised it would be the last time.

Right.

And those assholes believed her, so his childhood had been nothing but a pitiful merry-go-round from hell.

At least, it was until he turned fifteen.

Chapter 9

Sean hung up his phone and turned to Lynch. "That was my profiler. She'll be here in about ten minutes."

The detective nodded. "Great. Maybe she can make some sense out of this fucking mess." He swept his hand toward the whiteboards containing all the information they had on the case with a frustrated sigh.

Just after Brian and Rafe walked into the conference room, a few minutes later, one of the landline phones on the table rang. The front desk deputy reported that Dr. Suki Ralston had arrived. Sean headed out to greet her and escort her back to the task force room. He found her in the lobby, looking as gorgeous as ever, and he almost rolled his eyes as he thought of what his brother's response to this woman was going to be. Brian could be a dog when it came to women—love 'em and leave 'em—quickly. While Sean wouldn't mind having a long-term relationship with the right woman, Brian ran from commitment faster than anyone could say, "Ready, set, go."

Suki wore a dark blue suit with a skirt that stopped just above the knee. A crisp, white dress shirt, with the top two buttons undone, and three-inch, navy heels completed the outfit. Since the doctor spent most of her time in an office formulating profiles rather than actually chasing down criminals, she could get away with the high heels. But since she was also an agent, he knew beneath her jacket was a holstered weapon. She wore a gold chain around her neck, a simple wrist-watch, and minimal makeup. Suki didn't need much accessorizing to turn heads. Her jet-black hair was pulled up into a professional bun, but Sean knew when she let it down, it would fall to the middle of her back.

As he opened the door to let her into the back hall-way, her face lit up when she saw him. "Hey, stud muffin, how's that rhythm thing going?"

Sean grimaced. "Um, do me a favor, will you? My brother's working with us, so if you could cool it with the 'stud muffin' remarks, I'd really appreciate it."

"No problem. I know what it's like to be teased by older brothers." As they walked side-by-side down the hallway, she became serious and professional—as expected. "Has anything changed in the case since yesterday?"

He sighed heavily. "Yeah, we found three more victims in Philadelphia from last summer. The lead agent is sending the file down tonight—said she knows you... Karen Winslow?"

"Oh, yes, I know her well. She can be a little gruff at times, but she's an excellent agent."

"Well, anyway, now we have six vics, and we're still spinning our wheels. I'm hoping between you and Winslow, you can at least point us in some sort of direction."

"I'll do my best."

Sean opened the door to the conference room and let Suki walk in first, carrying her well-worn, brown leather briefcase. The four detectives, who had only seconds ago been in the middle of a conversation, suddenly fell silent as the petite woman entered the room and strode confidently to the head of the table. "Good afternoon, gentlemen."

There was a split second of hesitation before the men stood, almost as one, and returned her greeting. Sean made the introductions, indicating each person with a flash of his hand. "Suki, this is our lead detective, Brad Lynch, Rafe Montoya of the SBI, and my brother, Brian, also with the state police. Guys, this is Dr. Suki Ralston, FBI agent and profiler extraordinaire."

Suki shook hands with each man, seemingly oblivious to their teenage reactions to her natural beauty. When not working, she was a fun woman to be around, but when duty called, she was nothing but professional.

She reached over to pull out a chair, but a nearly-drooling Rafe, who'd been standing nearby, beat her to it, gesturing for her to sit. She smiled at him as she sat down. "Okay, gentlemen, please have a seat and tell me about this case from the start. Sean gave me the basics yesterday, but I'd like to hear everything from the top, including any theories you might have."

She opened her briefcase and pulled out a pen and a fresh, yellow legal-sized pad. Over the next hour, as each member of the task force spoke, Suki took copious amounts of notes, filling at least fifteen pages. She'd taken a shorthand class as an easy elective in high school and could write almost as fast as the men could talk—a talent that helped tremendously in her career.

When they finally finished filling her in, Sean added, "I also made you a copy of everything we have. I figured you'd be up late going through it all."

He handed her a heavy folder filled with a thick stack of papers, which she dropped next to her pad of notes. She lifted the top cover and scanned the first few pages. "Is there anything in here about the Philadelphia cases?"

"Winslow emailed me some stuff. It's in there. She's overnighting the rest, including an initial profile."

Suki glanced at Sean with raised eyebrows. "Who did the profile?"

He shrugged his shoulders. "Don't know, didn't ask. She wanted you at the time, but you weren't available."

She returned her attention to the file. "What about the autopsy reports and photos of your three vics, are they in here too?"

Rafe handed her three more manila files. "Here they are, Dr. Ralston. You should have the reports included with everything Sean gave you, but here are the autopsy and crime scene photos." He grimaced and added apologetically, "I'm sure you've seen a lot of nasty stuff working for the feds, but these are more than just a little disturbing. You can hold onto them if needed—the official ones are on a CD."

"Thank you, Detective, but as you know, 'disturbing' comes with the job."

"I hear you. And feel free to call me Rafe. We're pretty informal around here."

Suki smiled warmly. "Thanks, Rafe. And everyone, please call me Suki. My dad's an internist, and every time I hear Dr. Ralston, I look around to see where he is."

Her gaze met each one of the members of the task force in succession. "Thank you all for the update. I'll spend the next few hours reviewing the files and should have a preliminary profile for you in the morning or noon at the latest."

Brian and Rafe stood and said their goodbyes for the day, although the latter seemed reluctant to do so. The guy hadn't been able to take his gaze off Suki. But they needed to check in with their own supervisor. Even though they were on the serial-killer task force, they still had other cases to work on. Until the team had some more information or a lead or two, there wasn't much else the two agents could do at the sheriff's department.

Brian gave his brother a fist bump and a wink before walking out the door.

After they left, Suki began perusing the files as Lynch entered updates to existing reports on the department computer. Sean opened his laptop and signed on. Once he was in the right database, he expanded the parameters for a new search in the FBI system and hit send.

While the program was doing its thing, he strolled down the hall to the break room and put money in the soda machine. He grabbed two Cokes for Brad and himself and a Diet Coke for Suki, which was her usual. Sean often joked with his uncle that caffeine and sugar were the "breakfast, lunch, and dinner of champions" for almost anyone in law enforcement—they kept you going while doing the boring grunt work.

Lynch had told them earlier that it was his wife's birthday and he wanted to leave on time to take her out to dinner. Around five-thirty, he finished up, said goodbye, and headed out the door, leaving the two FBI agents alone in the room.

Suki stood and gracefully stretched her neck and back. "Speaking of dinner, you owe me, and I'm getting hungry."

He grinned at her. "When are you not hungry? For a tiny woman, you eat like a linebacker."

Laughing, she gathered up her files to place in her briefcase. "I wouldn't say a linebacker... maybe a wide receiver." She shrugged. "What can I say? I was blessed with a good metabolism. Now, where's this Sassy's Restaurant you've told me all about?"

* * *

Grace flipped through the local newspaper while standing behind the counter of Petals, her aunt's boutique. The women's clothing shop was a few doors down from Dan Malone's hardware store and diagonally across from Pro-Care. Bonnie was counting the day's receipts and chatting at the same time. "The warm weather this past week has had a nice effect on my sales. People are taking walks through town and getting ready for spring."

"Well, since March twentieth was last week, it's already spring," Grace responded. "Down here, you start getting the warmer weather way before New York does. Over a week of temperatures in the low seventies in March is almost unheard of up there. One or two days, maybe, but not nine in a row. This would be considered a heat wave."

"Are you complaining?"

She chuckled. "Absolutely not. This is my favorite type of weather, not too hot, not too cold."

"Mine too," said Bonnie. "And not just because it's good for business, but of course, that's a plus. I had a busy morning, and then a pleasant group of women came in after I returned from lunch. They drove down from Newport News for the day just to eat, shop, and walk around. And boy, did they shop!"

"Shopping is one thing." Grace raised an eyebrow. "The question is, did they buy?"

"Between the four of them, they bought over twelve hundred dollars' worth of clothing and accessories. I told them I was expecting a large shipment of summer clothes within the next two weeks, and they plan to come back down to see what comes in."

After she finished totaling up the sales, Bonnie put the credit card receipts into an envelope and filed them away, so she could compare them to the statements at the end of the month. Then she wrote out a bank slip and placed it with two days' worth of money and checks into a deposit bag that she concealed in a small shopping bag. She planned on dropping it into the night deposit bin at her bank, a block and a half away. Usually, Dan, taking along his concealed .38 caliber pistol and Jinx, walked with her every time she went to the bank to make his own deposits and to ensure Bonnie wasn't robbed. Even though crime in Whisper was low, one never knew when some creep would try to take advantage of someone in the sleepy little town, he would say.

Bonnie always thought her dear friend was overly

cautious but let him play bodyguard anyway. Dan randomly chose when they would make the deposits, so there was no pattern to catch a crook's eye. Sometimes they went in the morning before opening their shops, and other times they went during lunch or after closing. Tonight, though, Grace and she would make the drop on their way to dinner.

It was still a few minutes before the six o'clock closing time, so the two women straightened the clothes on the racks. Bonnie asked, "Did you hire that therapist you told me about at lunch? What's his name again?"

"Tom Koppel. And yes, I did. He's giving the hospital his two weeks' notice on Monday."

"Wonderful. So you're almost ready to open up then?"

Grace smiled. "Yup, as soon as all the equipment arrives. The sign looks great—they're installing it on Tuesday. Oh, and I bought the TV earlier to put up for the patients to watch if they want. It was so nice of Dan to offer to mount it on the wall, run the wiring, and hook up the washer/dryer for me. That'll save me some money. I think I'll treat him to dinner out one night to pay him back."

"Well, not tonight. That stubborn old coot's been fighting a cold for the past few days, and now he's paying the price. Thank goodness Jimmy Merrick was scheduled to work after school today, so Dan could go up to the apartment and get some rest.

Honestly, that man pushes himself to the brink sometimes."

Grace smiled and again wondered why Dan and Bonnie weren't a couple. It was obvious they cared about each other, and most of the time, they acted like old married folks. "We'll bring him some soup from Sassy's after dinner."

"Sounds perfect." Bonnie glanced at her watch. "Well, let's lock up. I'm getting hungry myself."

The two women closed the shop and walked up the street to the bank. While Bonnie was making the deposit, Grace glanced across the street just in time to see Sean walking into Sassy's with his hand on the lower back of an extremely attractive woman. She was stunned and felt her stomach fall in disappointment. She suddenly realized that in the conversations she'd had with Sean over the past week, she had never once asked him if he was seeing anyone special. Apparently, he was, she thought sourly as the couple disappeared into the restaurant.

Bonnie completed her transaction and turned to see her niece frowning. "Is something wrong, Grace?" she asked while scanning the area in front of Sassy's where her niece had been staring.

"Um, no. Nothing's wrong," she lied and put on a fake smile. "I was just thinking that I'm really not in the mood for Sassy's tonight. Why don't we drive over to the Cranberry Inn for dinner?"

"That's fine with me. I haven't eaten there in a while."

* * *

"...this is Jessica Daly for the Channel Four News."

Wallace rewound the reporter's newscast from outside the Dare County Sheriff's Department and let it play for the fifth time. He could tell she was full of herself and wondered if she'd be so cocky if he cut her down to size. Literally.

Here comes the best part. The FBI agent. Mister High and Mighty—Not.

His deadly work had the local *Keystone Kops* running around in circles, so they'd called in the feds. It didn't matter, though—they were a bunch of inept jackasses and would never catch him.

Good ol' George Wallace had a steady, respectable job, helped out his neighbors, and was friendly to everyone he met—well, almost everyone. His coworkers and boss got along with him just fine, and he'd never had any complaints lodged against him at work. He'd never been arrested—even his driver's license was clean, having never gotten a ticket in his life. He even volunteered every other Saturday afternoon at the local food pantry and drove his elderly neighbor to the library once a month. It was all part of the admirable persona he presented to the rest of the world. People who knew him had no idea what he was capable of, and he would keep it that way. Of course, it was a tad disappointing that no one knew that mild-mannered George Wallace was responsible for instilling fear in the hearts of women in the area, but, ironically, silence ensured his fame.

Striding into his kitchen, he took his dinner out of the microwave and placed it on a tray along with a knife, fork, and napkin. He carried his meal into the living room, sat back down on the sofa, and hit the rewind button on the remote again.

Chapter 10

Grace glanced around the almost full dining room of the Cranberry Inn. Named for its exterior color, it was a beautiful bed and breakfast on the north end of town, which opened its doors to the public from five until nine for supper. The Victorian décor matched the architecture of the grand building and inspired a different atmosphere than Sassy's did. The restaurant on Main Street was always fun, loud, and boisterous, with the bar area having its regular crowd due to a row of TVs showing current sporting events. The dining area was a little quieter, yet it was still filled with happy chatter. Here at the inn, the environment was more subdued, and most conversations were carried out in soft, delicate voices.

Bonnie gave a small wave across the room to one of her regular customers before returning her attention to her dinner companion. "Are you all right, Gracie?

You're awfully quiet, and you've barely touched your dinner."

She stopped moving her penne ala vodka around the plate and sighed. "I'm fine, Aunt Bonnie. Guess I wasn't that hungry after all."

She couldn't tell her aunt she was upset because the night after he'd kissed the stuffing out of her, she saw Sean out on a date with another woman. It felt like Mary Jo Schreiber and the prom all over again—only worse. "I'll take it home for lunch tomorrow."

Bonnie was a smart cookie. She knew something was bothering her niece, but Grace could be as stubborn as a mule. The older woman would wait until Grace was willing to open up about it. Instead of pushing her to talk, Bonnie waved down their waitress and requested a container of the cook's delicious chicken and rice soup to go.

Grace drove Bonnie back to Main Street, where she would deliver the soup to Dan's apartment, above his hardware store, before going home. After making sure her aunt got inside okay, Grace steered her car west. As she passed Sassy's, she slowed the vehicle down, looking for Sean's Mustang. She didn't know whether she was disappointed when she didn't see it.

Shaking her head, she told herself it shouldn't bother her that he was out with another woman. They'd shared a few meals together since they'd both returned to Whisper, but those hadn't actually been dates—just spur-of-the-moment get-togethers. It wasn't as if she had any claim on the man. The kiss they'd shared had obviously meant more to her than it did to him.

Well, she wasn't the type of woman who liked to share. If Sean wanted to date other women, that was his choice, but Grace wouldn't sit around waiting for him. Once her business was up and running, she would find a way to meet new people. For now, she'd have to be content with the few she knew in the area.

"Maybe tomorrow I'll go to the shelter and adopt a kitten. At least that would be something I could cuddle up with," she said out loud, trying to convince herself that would be enough.

Entering her silent condo finalized her decision. She was going to get a cat. She'd had one when she was little and missed having a furry companion to come home to—someone, or in this case, something to talk to at night when she was alone.

Turning on the lights, she dropped her bag, hung up her coat, and slid her shoes off. The remaining portion of her dinner went into the refrigerator, and then she strode to her bedroom to put on her pajamas. After getting comfortable on the couch, with a few magazines Bonnie had given her, she turned on the television and waited for the ten o'clock news to come on.

* * *

Sean showed Suki to her bedroom in the beach house, then went into his own room to change out of his suit as she settled in. A few minutes later, he walked out to the living room and glanced at his watch. It was a quarter to ten, but he knew they would be up for a few more hours going through the case reports.

He'd already read the printouts from Philadelphia but would do it again to see if he'd missed anything. Plopping down on the couch, he wondered if it was too late to call Grace. They would have been home earlier, but he'd forgotten to bring his laptop, and they'd returned to the station, where it was locked in the conference room.

Standing, he grabbed his cell phone from the dining table and found Grace's number in his contacts. She'd given it to him the night before as they sat on the couch talking. Leaning against the door jamb between the living room and kitchen, he pressed send and hoped he wasn't about to wake her up. It rang a few times before going to voicemail, and he disconnected the call before leaving a message because he wasn't sure what he wanted to say.

"Got a girlfriend you haven't told me about?" Suki teased as she walked into the room wearing a T-shirt and sweatpants. She strode over to the porch door where she'd left her briefcase on the floor when they first entered the cottage. Grabbing the leather handles, she carried it to the loveseat, which faced the windows overlooking the ocean, and sat down.

Sean shrugged and tossed his phone on the couch. "To tell you the truth, I'm not sure."

"Want to talk about it?" Sean had mentioned Grace several times over dinner, and it was obvious to Suki that the woman had caught his interest.

"No, thanks." He honestly didn't because he wouldn't know where to start, so he changed the subject. "We're going to be up for a while, aren't we?"

"I know I am, why?"

Sean smiled and rubbed his hands together. "I've been looking for an excuse to start a fire in the fireplace. What do you say?" He pointed at the stack of dry wood set neatly to the right of the brick hearth. Although the days had been warm, the nights were still chilly, especially on the beach.

"Great. I'd love it." She stood and stepped toward the kitchen. "You wouldn't happen to have some hot chocolate in here, would you? Can't have a fire without some cocoa."

"Look in the cabinet next to the fridge." He began putting some logs and crumpled newspaper into the fireplace. "There should be some for the Keurig machine. Make mine a cappuccino, please."

"Sure thing. By the way," she said, turning around to face him from the doorway, "you never told me you were working with a bunch of hunky guys on this. You could have warned me, you know."

Sean rolled his eyes. "Sorry, but checking out guys for you is not my thing." He paused and peered at her over his shoulder. "Which one caught your eye?" He didn't really want to know, but curiosity got the best of him.

"I'm not sure yet, but when I figure it out, you'll be the second one to know." Suki raised her eyebrows several times in rapid succession and chuckled. "Maybe the third."

Sean laughed and shook his head at the profiler—she was a hoot. Ten minutes later, the fire was roaring, and they were sipping their drinks. Both were immersed in their individual files—Sean on the sofa, Suki on the loveseat. She continued to make notes on her pad, and Sean knew her well enough not to interrupt her as she created the profile. He'd have to wait until morning and hear her analysis along with everyone else.

Around midnight, his eyes were blurry and watery from so much reading. Standing, he shuffled over to the hearth and secured a metal cover to the front of the fireplace. The fire had faded down to glowing embers because he'd been too engrossed in his reading to stoke it.

He sat back down and stretched out, leaning his head on the back of the couch, thinking of Grace. He wanted to ask her out on an official date since they hadn't been on one yet. Maybe he should talk to Uncle Dan and see if he thought it was a good idea. Sean hadn't asked the older man for advice on women since he was a teenager, but Grace was special. It was something he felt in his gut. The woman was *damn* special.

Closing his eyes, he thought about those wicked, hazel eyes and her blonde hair. He loved it when she took down her ponytail, as she had the night before. Her hair was long and straight, making him want to wrap it around his hand and wrist and pull her to him. She had been dressed in jeans or sweats the few times he had seen her, and he wondered what they were hiding. If he invited her to the Cranberry Inn, maybe she'd wear a dress or a skirt. He'd bet everything he owned her legs were fucking knockouts.

His mind wandered as he imagined those legs wrapped around him as he entered her, kissing and nuzzling her neck and shoulders as he eased himself further into her hot, wet pussy. He could almost feel the weight of her breasts as he kneaded them with his hands—her skin silky and soft. God, she was fucking beautiful. He heard her murmur in his ear, "Hey, hot stuff, wake up."

Huh? Something wasn't right. Cracking his eyes open, he found himself lying on his side on the couch, a blanket over the lower half of his body, and Suki standing over him, drinking a cup of coffee. She was dressed in a brown suit with a pale blue blouse. "Wake up, sleepyhead, it's almost seven."

Sean glanced over to the windows and saw the sun was up.

Holy shit.

He'd fallen asleep on the couch and slept there all night. Thankfully, he realized something else was up before he removed the blanket. Dragging his hand down his face, he tried to get his morning wood under control. Suki was a good friend, but she certainly didn't need to see him in such an aroused state.

Oblivious to his dilemma, she headed back toward the kitchen. "You looked so comfortable last night, so I just threw the blanket on you around one when I went to bed. Go hop in the shower while I make you a cup of coffee. Should I find us something to eat, or do you want to grab something on the way in?"

Sean took advantage of her facing away from him, jumped up, and headed to his bedroom. "Something on the way is fine. There's a decent bagel place in town."

"Sounds good to me."

After showering and getting dressed, Sean grabbed his computer, files, and the travel mug of coffee Suki had filled for him. She'd found two of them in the cabinets and loaded them both up for the ride into the station. Carrying her briefcase and coffee, she followed Sean out to his Mustang. They'd left her rental car at the station last night since they'd been together anyway, and both of them needed to be back at the sheriff's department by eight this morning. Pulling out of the driveway, he steered toward town.

Still pissed off about Sean, Grace tried to push him from her mind as she stood in line for breakfast at Bagel Bonanza on Main Street, just up from her shop. She'd tossed and turned half the night, imagining him with that other woman. What annoyed her even more was every time she closed her eyes, she remembered the kiss they'd shared and how her body had come to life in those few seconds as she'd slowly melted against him. When her nipples had brushed against his hard chest, she'd been shocked at the jolt of electricity that had shot through her, straight to her core. While she'd been disappointed when he left instead of kissing her again —or taking her to bed as he'd mentioned—she was grateful now that's how the evening had ended.

After paying for her bagel and coffee, she headed for the door. It opened before she reached it, and she almost walked right into Sean... and *her*. Grace's eyes grew wide when she saw him, then narrowed slightly at the sight of the petite woman standing beside him.

"Grace! Hi!" Sean grinned.

Really? Didn't the man have any fucking shame?

"Hi, Sean." She hoped she sounded indifferent. She'd be damned if she'd let him know how hurt she was.

It was just after seven thirty in the morning, and he was still with the woman he had dinner with last night. It didn't take a fucking genius to figure out they'd spent the night together. Look at him, she thought, he's blushing— obviously embarrassed he'd run into her on the heels of last night's date. She couldn't decide if she wanted to punch him or be swallowed into a black hole and disappear.

Suddenly, the other woman did something that shocked Grace—she smiled, stuck out her hand, and happily introduced herself. "Hi, Grace, I'm Suki Ralston. I work with Sean. He told me all about you last night. I hear you're opening a business nearby. Congratulations."

It took Grace a long moment to respond. This was not what she'd expected—she'd already decided she wanted to hate the other woman, maybe even wanted to scratch her eyes out. But Suki was looking her straight in the eye as if she knew exactly what Grace was thinking, and yet she was still attempting to be friendly.

Grace slowly reached out and shook the proffered hand, still very confused. "Um... yes, I am. You... um... you work with Sean?"

The man in question was the one who answered her. "Actually, Suki has a doctorate in criminal psychology. She's a profiler based out of Quantico and came to help us out. We've been friends for a couple of years."

"Oh," Grace responded in a flat tone of voice, unsure of how she should react to that information.

Suki must have sensed her continuing uncertainty because she added, "We're *just* friends—nothing more. Now, why don't I grab a bunch of bagels for the rest of the task force while you two talk?" She winked at Grace and then made her way over to the counter to order.

Grace stared openmouthed at Suki as she strode past.

"Grace? You okay?" Sean asked with concern in his voice.

She turned back toward him. Moaning, she brought her hands to her burning cheeks. "I'm such an idiot."

Now it was Sean's turn to be confused. His eyes narrowed. "What are you talking about?"

He took one of her hands and led her to a small, empty table so they wouldn't block the doorway for a few people who were leaving.

Grace swallowed hard before her words rushed out. "I saw the two of you walking into Sassy's last night and just assumed you were on a date. And when you walked in here with the same woman, I figured you'd spent the night together. And you have no idea how embarrassed I am right now."

"*Ah.*" Sean laughed, fueling her mortification. "Is that why you didn't answer your phone last night?" She nodded, her gaze pinned to his broad chest to avoid looking him in the face. "Well, to tell you the truth, Suki is borrowing a spare bedroom at the beach house. But we are not and have never been romantically involved. As she said, we're good friends, and I thought she'd be more comfortable staying at the cottage than at a hotel."

With two fingers of his right hand under her chin, he tilted her head up so their eyes met. "I hope you're not mad."

"Mad? No! Just very, *very* embarrassed. I'm sorry. I mean, we aren't even dating, but after that kiss the other night..." She paused, swallowed hard, and took the plunge. "Well, I guess I was kind of hoping..."

His face lit up, and he let out a low chuckle that was incredibly sexy. "If you must know, I was kind of hoping too." He brushed back a strand of hair that had fallen forward onto her cheek, and she felt the brief heat of his fingers on her skin. "Listen, I don't know how busy I'll be today, but is it all right if I call you later?"

Chapter 11

The task force settled down with their cups of coffee and bagels, preparing for Suki's presentation. She took a sip of the coffee she'd refilled in the department's break room and grimaced. Sean knew how she felt. In his seven years working for the FBI, he had yet to find a decent cup of liquid caffeine in any of the police stations he'd visited. He knew she was missing her own supply of expensive, gourmet coffee she kept in her office—she was a self-admitted connoisseur and snob of a good brew.

Glancing at the group of men seated around the table, she took a deep breath and began her report. "I've read through the files and autopsy reports and believe I've come up with a pretty accurate profile on your killer."

"How accurate is accurate?" Rafe asked. It was evident to Sean that the detective was not only interested in the profiler as a woman but also respected her professional input.

"Well, with profiling, there's always room for adjustment. It's an ongoing process that evolves with each kill and crime scene. I may need to tweak my analysis a little when I get hold of the entire Philadelphia case file. However, I believe I'm about ninety percent accurate with this one."

She stood and began pacing the room. Sean knew it was a habit she found helped her thought process. "You're looking for a male in his late thirties or forties with average or just above average intelligence and educational level. He'll be able to blend in with his surroundings and is probably considered a model citizen by many. His neighbors have nothing bad to say about him. He holds a good job and may even be married to, or dating, a woman who's the opposite of his victims.

"In other words, a shy, dark-haired, plain Jane who wears frumpy or old-fashioned clothes. He probably comes from a single-parent home and was raised by an abusive mother. Something set him off in Philadelphia, and because the first victim there was a prostitute and he's carving the word 'slut' into them, my guess is the victim propositioned him.

"His first kill surprised him—it wasn't something he planned. From the initial report we received, it seemed to be a disorganized kill—he didn't try to revive her after strangling her, and the carved torso was done postmortem. However, when it was all over, he realized he enjoyed it—it turned him on. He gained more and more confidence with each kill and, as a result, became more organized. And now, with the publicity, it's possible he'll increase the frequency of his kills."

Lynch's eyes widened. "You mean he's not going to wait a month?"

The doctor shook her head. "I don't think so. He's had a taste of fame now, and he's going to enjoy it."

"Great. That's just fucking great." Brad brought his fingers to his temples and rubbed them. "We may have a profile now, but it brings us no fucking closer to catching this asshole. That description could be any one of the hundreds of thousands of men in the county."

"That may be," Sean replied, "but at least if we start coming up with suspects, we can narrow them down."

"I think these women have all been victims of opportunity," Suki continued. "I don't believe he stalked them, and the first time he met them was the night he killed them."

Sean leaned back in his chair, flipping a pen through his fingers. "So he went looking for a certain type of woman, found one, and zeroed right in on her. The first five victims were all placed where they would be found relatively quickly. Why was Daphne Jones further off the beaten path, literally?"

"Could be something as simple as he got spooked.

Maybe while he was disposing of the body in the park, he heard someone coming and had to hide."

"Okay," Brian interjected, "here's another question. Why the three kills in Pennsylvania, one each month, then nothing until he started up again down here? They obviously had no suspects there, and it hadn't hit the media. He wasn't about to be discovered, so why move down here? Why not stay where he was having, I hate to say it, success? It's not like he ran out of victims."

Suki shrugged her shoulders. "I don't think his move to North Carolina had anything to do with his kills, his victims, or a chance of being discovered. Maybe his job transferred him, or he moved due to family reasons. As long as he has a large pool of victims to choose from, it really doesn't matter where he lives."

"Hopefully, he'll start screwing up somewhere and give us a lead because right now, we've got nothing." Sean turned on his laptop, checked his emails, and found one from Mark Evans, the tech at the FBI lab who was running the DNA. He opened the message and then told the rest of the task force what it entailed. "Mark put a rush on the DNA for me. As I expected, it didn't match anybody in the system. However, if we come up with a suspect, at least we have a sample to compare to."

He glanced at Lynch. "Have we gotten anything on the tip line yet?"

The man sighed in frustration. "Fuck, yeah. I

haven't listened to them yet, but I checked just before I came in here, and there were a hundred and forty-two messages. It'll take me an hour or two to listen to them all. When I'm done, we can split them up and start weeding out the crazies. Doc, do you have anything else for us?"

Pulling out her chair, Suki sat down. "The only other thing is the pennies. I agree with Sean's theory that the 1993 date has some sort of significance for the UNSUB, but what that is, we may never know unless he tells us. That's pretty much it, but I may have more after I receive the rest of the files from Philadelphia."

"In that case, I'm going to update Griffin, then start on that list of tips."

After Brad left the room, Sean finished browsing on his laptop. "There are no other hits on the parameters I entered into the system. It looks like Philadelphia was his starting point. Now we have to figure out why."

For the next hour, Sean and Suki reviewed the case files again, along with their notes, while Brian and Rafe added the profile and other info to the whiteboards. Just after nine-thirty, an FBI courier arrived with the Philadelphia case files. The two federal agents dug in and began looking for something that could possibly lead them to a suspect. Meanwhile, the state agents went to get a list of tips from Brad to start exploring.

Around three o'clock, Sean stepped out into the hallway and took a moment to call Grace. She answered her phone on the second ring, and he was surprised at how pleased he was just to hear her voice.

"Hi, Sean, how's your day going?"

"Much better now that I'm speaking to you. How about you? Was everything delivered on time?"

Grace let out a little laugh. "Yes, the delivery truck showed up at ten o'clock. I now have my chairs, the PT tables, and the washer/dryer. Since there was nothing else to do over there today, I've been helping Bonnie out at the boutique."

"Great. Listen, Suki will only be here for one more night, and I wanted to invite you over for dinner, so you could get to know her. She's a great person, and I think you two would really like each other. I was going to grab some steaks and throw them on the grill. So what do you say?"

"That sounds good, and I guess I owe her an apology for this morning," she said wryly.

"I wouldn't worry about that—I'm sure she's already forgotten all about it. We should be out of here by five, and we'll stop at the grocery store on the way home. Why don't you meet us at the beach house at six?"

"Why don't I save you the trouble and go to the grocery store myself? I'll meet you around five thirty then."

"If you don't mind, that'd be great. I'll call if we're going to be late. Otherwise, I'll see you at five-thirty."

Sean hung up the phone as Suki exited the ladies'

room and stopped in front of him. "Are you sure you don't mind me staying one more night?"

"Not at all. I'd really like you to get to know Grace anyway."

"I like her already—I think she's good for you."

A wide grin spread across his face. "So do I. Let's get back to work and catch this fucker so I can spend the rest of my vacation getting to know her a lot better."

* * *

Jessica Daly hung up the phone and smiled. Her source at the sheriff's department had come through, and she would out-scoop her competition again. By the time those gun-toting imbeciles caught this killer, she'd be in a prime position to demand another raise at the network. Maybe she'd even get the coveted anchor position on the six o'clock news she'd been working toward her whole career.

If she could get her hands on everything the detectives had, she'd probably be able to solve the case herself. She had great investigative instincts and a talent for getting people to talk. Over the past few years, her list of informants had grown to the point she could get information no matter what it was or who it involved. Most of her contacts were men—men who were so predictable. Show a little cleavage, and the floodgates that were their mouths opened up and poured forth.

Sitting at her desk in the newsroom, she glanced at the wall clock. It was just after three in the afternoon, which only gave her an hour or so before she had to be in front of the camera and tape her report in time for the 5:30 p.m. deadline. First things first, though—she called cameraman Marty Kendall and told him to get his gear ready and meet her at the news van at three-forty-five sharp.

"And don't make me wait for you this time," she barked before hanging up. Jessica hated slackers on the job, and Marty was always late. Sometimes, she thought he did it on purpose, but soon, that wouldn't matter—this serial killer was her ticket off the street and into the anchor chair.

She tried to decide where she wanted to film her brief—in front of the sheriff's department, the medical examiner's office, the last crime scene, or the bar where Daphne Jones disappeared from. Which would have the largest impact? With the information she'd just gained from her source, she opted for the ME's office. Turning on her computer, she typed exactly what she wanted to say. This was going to be big, she told herself —bigger than big—it would be fucking *huge*.

At ten after four, they pulled into the parking lot of the municipal building that housed the Dare County medical examiner's office. The weather was still warm and slightly overcast, but Jessica found this was the best lighting for her when filming outdoors. She thought she looked too pale on TV when it was bright and sunny out. She flipped down the passenger's visor to fix her hair and makeup.

Marty parked the van, and as he started to hop out, she snapped, "Hurry and get everything set. I want this filmed and ready for the top of the six." Having the lead story on the evening news was something all the street reporters fought over, and tonight, it would be a no-brainer with Jessica's story.

Marty mumbled something she didn't hear and, truthfully, didn't care about. He may be slow and lazy, but when it came to actually filming, he was the best cameraman they had, and that was all that mattered to her. As long as she looked good on her newscasts, she could put up with all the other bullshit that came with him.

After adding the extra makeup needed for the camera, Jessica climbed out of the van and strode to the front of the building, leaving Marty to haul the camera and microphone over. She looked at several different angles of the entrance before choosing to stand just to the left of the Dare County Medical Examiner sign.

Glancing over her shoulder, she saw Marty taking his sweet time walking toward her. "Hurry up, will you? I want to make sure we get this right."

Marty muttered "bitch" under his breath and refused to walk any faster. He hated working with Jessica, and the feeling was mutual, but he was the best cameraman they had, so she insisted that he be the one to film her. He'd tried to get rid of her by going to his boss to complain. His supervisor had told him that there was nothing he could do about it. He just had to suck it up. As long as he did his job, Jessica couldn't care less about his opinion of her.

"Stand over there—I want this angle." She pointed to where she wanted him to set up as he handed her the microphone, which had CH4 in large print on the side. Whether he liked her or not, she was a damn good reporter and knew how to choose the right places to film. He had already received two awards for excellence in filming thanks to her, not that he ever had shown her any gratitude.

Hoisting the camera to his shoulder, he made a few final adjustments and then gave Jessica the signal to start whenever she was ready. She straightened her back and shoulders, put her "serious reporter" face on, and held the microphone just below her chin. "This is Jessica Daly for the evening news, reporting to you from the Dare County Medical Examiner's Office with a Channel Four exclusive.

"Investigations into the strangling deaths of three county women continue. At this time, local law enforcement has very few leads. Sources inside the Dare County Sheriff's Department report..."

Chapter 12

After speaking to Sean on the phone, Grace strolled down to the hardware store to see Dan. It was nothing new to step over a snoring Jinx as she entered the shop—the sunlit area was the dog's favorite spot to sleep. All of the store's regular customers knew to check the threshold before walking in to avoid tripping over the big lug.

The older Malone was still fighting his cold but, as always, was too stubborn to slow down. She was happy to hear he was feeling a little better and seemed to be getting his energy back. Jimmy, the college student who worked for him part-time, was picking up extra hours so Dan could at least go upstairs to his apartment for a nap before returning to close the shop at six.

Grace explained to him that she was joining Sean and Suki for dinner and asked to borrow the key to the beach house, so she could start making dinner if the other two were running late. Dan gave her a spare and told her to keep it.

"Are you sure, Dan?"

"You may not be blood-related, but you're still family," he replied with a grin. "Feel free to use the cottage anytime you want."

She kissed him on his cheek, then laughed when he asked, "What was that for?"

"For considering me part of your family. It's very sweet of you."

Blushing, he waved his hand at her. "Well, it's true. You're the niece I never had."

Grace made a spur-of-the-moment decision. "Can I ask you something, Dan? It's personal, so you can tell me it's none of my business if you want."

"Okay, shoot."

"You lost your wife at such a young age. I know it must have been hard in the beginning, but didn't you ever think of getting married again?"

Dan smiled warmly. "I only had two wonderful years with Annie. You know, we eloped after knowing each other for only a few weeks." Grace smiled and nodded. "And you're right, it was very tough at first—I thought we'd grow old together, but fate threw us a nasty curveball. Thankfully, I had family and friends who made sure I didn't bury myself right along with her. I was still in my late twenties then. Before she died, Annie made me promise that someday I'd date again."

Leaning against the counter, Grace raised her brow. "And did you?"

He shrugged, fiddling with a display of fishing lures he kept in stock for the local anglers. "Here and there, starting a few years after I lost her. I just never found anyone special. Why do you ask?"

"I don't know—just curious, I guess." She was suddenly hesitant to ask about his and Bonnie's relationship, so she changed the direction of her questioning. "When you first met Annie, when did you know she was 'the one,' and how?"

"Now that's easy." His face lit up. "The moment I saw her face the day we met, I knew. Not sure how I knew, but it was almost like my guardian angel was sitting on my shoulder saying, 'That's your future wife, in case you were wondering.'"

Grace laughed. "Really?"

"Really. Now, who's caught those pretty, hazel eyes of yours, hmm?"

"Nobody!" But she answered too fast and too vehemently to convince the old man, and he just raised his eyebrows at her. She felt her cheeks redden. "That obvious, huh?"

Dan nodded and tilted his head. "It wouldn't happen to be my nephew by chance?"

She didn't even have to ask which nephew he was referring to. "At first, I just thought it was my teenage crush coming back..."

"But you're no longer a teenager," he finished for her.

"Exactly. Please don't say anything to Sean... or Aunt Bonnie, for that matter. I'm not sure what's going on between us just yet. I mean, we've had a good time this past week, but it's not like we're dating."

"Well, I won't say anything to Sean, but your aunt already figured out something was going on between the two of you," Dan informed her. When Grace's eyes widened at his statement, he laughed. "Come on, we might be old, but we're not blind."

Grace chuckled. "No, I guess you're not." She gave him another peck on the cheek. "And the two of you are not old, just much wiser than the rest of us."

By the time Sean and Suki arrived a little after five thirty, Grace already warmed up the grill and had three potatoes wrapped in foil cooking on it. As the profiler was in her bedroom changing out of her business attire, Sean stood in the kitchen with Grace. She loved how he looked in his suit with his tie loosened and the top button on his shirt undone. Leaning against the counter next to her, he looked like a male model on the cover of *GQ* magazine. With those bedroom eyes, the dimple on his left cheek, and those oh-so-kissable lips, ladies of the world, eat your hearts out!

"Thanks for going to the store for me," he said, stealing a slice of cucumber from the cutting board in front of her and popping it into his mouth.

She smiled and continued to cut the vegetables

she'd bought for a salad. "No problem. I had plenty of time to do it—you would have been in a rush."

He hesitated momentarily, then put his arm around Grace's waist, pulling her closer. When she didn't resist, he lowered his head and pressed his lips to hers. The electricity between them sparked to life again, only this time it was stronger and not a surprise like their first kiss. This time, they both knew it was coming and craved it. Grace dropped the knife she was using to cut tomatoes and ran her flat palms up Sean's chest and shoulders. God, how she loved the feel of him!

Grace felt her body start to hum from head to toe and everywhere in between. She'd been hoping for a chance to kiss him again, and here it was. He tasted sweet, like the Pinot grigio he had sipped, but with something else that was all Sean. He probed her lips with his tongue, silently begging her to open them and allow him access to her mouth. Grace was just about to do that when they heard, "Whoops, don't mind me."

They jumped apart at the sound of Suki's voice. She laughed and walked over to where the wine and a clean glass awaited her. "I said, 'Don't mind me.' Feel free to continue. I'm just grabbing a glass of wine and going into the living room. You two lovebirds just forget I'm here."

Blushing, Sean and Grace looked at each other and chuckled. They'd both forgotten there was someone else in the house, and if they hadn't been interrupted, things might have heated up very quickly.

Sean leaned forward and gave her a swift kiss on the lips. "I'm going to take a quick shower and change. Be right back."

"I'll be here," she responded with a sexy grin.

Grace finished the salad and heated some broccoli as Suki set the table. The large flat-screen TV above the fireplace was on channel four, and the evening news would start in about fifteen minutes.

"You know, Sean is really smitten with you," Suki said while she gathered up silverware from one of the kitchen drawers.

"The feeling is mutual." Her blush returned at the admission.

"I've known him a while and have never seen him this taken with a woman. I'm happy for both of you, but I'm also a little protective of him, so if you break his heart, I'll have to break your legs."

Grace's head whipped up to look at the other woman. She relaxed when she realized Suki was grinning.

"I'm kidding," Suki reassured her. "He's a tough guy and can take care of himself. I always thought the woman who won him over would be very lucky, but as I get to know you, I think he's the lucky one."

Grace wasn't sure why, but having the woman's approval felt good. "Thank you. But to tell you the truth, we haven't even been on a real date yet. I like him a lot but worry he doesn't feel the way I do. I mean, I don't do casual when it comes to relationships."

"And you're worried Sean just wants a fling?" She nodded, and Suki continued, "I can't speak for him, but I can tell you this—he is the happiest I've ever seen him, despite the case we're on. You're good for him, and I think he knows it."

As Suki left the kitchen, Grace thought about what the other woman had said and hoped she was right because being with Sean felt like where she belonged.

* * *

When Sean returned from his shower, dressed in a comfortable pair of faded jeans, black slippers, and a gray long-sleeved T-shirt, he found the two women chatting in the kitchen about a TV show. Happy they seemed to be getting along, he grabbed the plate of steaks Grace had prepared and headed down to the patio to throw them on the grill. It was a beautiful night out, cooler than it had been during the past week but clear and crisp. Stars already filled the sky, and a half-moon hung low in the east. He took a deep breath and savored the salty air. He loved this place, and now that he was home, he wondered why it had taken him so long to return for good.

He shut off the gas to the grill and was just putting the steaks and potatoes back on the plate when he heard the door up on the porch open. Suki's voice reached him. "Sean, you'd better get up here. We've got big trouble."

Gripping the plate tightly, he ran up the steps two at a time. Suki held the door open for him, and he entered, looking wildly for Grace, thinking she was hurt. But she was fine and standing behind the couch, staring at the TV. Confused, he looked at Suki. "What's wrong?"

"The news. Apparently, they have new information on our case—an exclusive. It's coming up next, and I don't think we're going to like it."

Sean set the plate of food on the dining table, strode over to the couch, and sat on the edge, leaning forward in anticipation. He picked up the remote and raised the volume a few notches. Grace came around and sat down next to him while Suki perched herself on the arm of the loveseat. They waited impatiently through two more commercials before the newscast started. The co-anchors introduced themselves and some of the upcoming stories before the male anchor announced, "But first, a Channel Four exclusive from our own Jessica Daly."

The picture switched from the news desk to an outdoor shot of the blonde reporter outside the Dare County Medical Examiner's Office. Sean immediately recognized her from the press conference. She wore a very serious expression as she began speaking.

"This is Jessica Daly for the evening news, reporting

to you from the Dare County Medical Examiner's Office with a Channel Four exclusive.

"Investigations into the strangling deaths of three county women continue. At this time, local law enforcement has very few leads. Sources inside the Dare County Sheriff's Department report the Seaside Strangler mutilated the torsos of his three victims with a knife before killing them. The word he carved into their abdomens is an expletive that cannot be repeated on television.

"Apparently, all three victims had been out partying with friends at different locations before encountering the vicious sadist who took their lives.

"This reporter has also discovered this is not the first time this savage has struck. The FBI was called in last summer by the Philadelphia Police Department after three women in three months were found strangled and with the same expletive cut into their torsos. That information was never made public, and no other homicides were reported. The killer apparently went into hiding until a little over two months ago, when Becky Travis was brutally murdered. Is this barbarian finished slaughtering the women of Dare County, or has he just begun?

"Channel Four is warning its female viewers to be extra vigilant and to use every precaution available to keep themselves safe.

"If anyone has any information regarding these

brutal crimes, please contact our tip line at Channel Four or the Dare County Sheriff's Department.

"This is Jessica Daly. Back to you, Ken."

"Son of a goddamned fucking bitch!" Sean roared as Suki took the remote control from him and lowered the TV volume again. After knowing him for over two years, she was surprised he waited until the end of the broadcast before blowing up. He was usually cool and in control, but when something like this set him off, look out. "Where the hell does this bitch get her fucking information?"

Since it was obvious the two women had no answer to his question, Sean stood and stormed into the kitchen to retrieve his cell phone. Locating Brad Lynch's number, he pressed send and paced back and forth in the small room. The phone only rang once before the call was answered. Without even saying hello, Lynch told him, "I just saw it. Who the fuck is she getting her information from?"

"That's what I want to know!" Sean bellowed into the phone. "The Seaside Strangler? Is she fucking kidding?"

Taking a deep breath, he lowered his voice, but the angry tone remained. "Brad, this isn't a slow leak anymore—this is going to cause a flood. The only thing not public now is the pennies."

"I know, I know. Shit, Griffin's cutting in. I'll talk to you in the morning. There's nothing we can do now." The detective clicked off as he took the other call.

Sean stopped pacing and found Grace and Suki staring at him from the kitchen doorway. As furious as he was, he realized Brad was right. There wasn't anything they could do about it now. By 11:00 p.m., every other news show would repeat what Jessica Daly had already reported. And first thing tomorrow morning, she would be getting a visit from the FBI—specifically, Special Agent Sean Malone.

Running his hands down his face, he brought his temper under control and pasted on a wry smile. "I can't do anything about it tonight, so we might as well go eat while it's still warm." Unfortunately, he'd lost his appetite.

* * *

That bitch! That slutty, little bitch! What had she called him? *A vicious sadist? A savage? A barbarian?* How dare she label him that way! The great George Wallace was none of those things. He was just a man ridding the world of despicable whores—someone had to. Those sluts deserved to die. Their promiscuous lifestyles had sealed their fates, just like that bitch on TV had sealed her own a moment ago. If she wanted to call him a savage, then he would gladly show her just how cruel he could be.

He slowly brought his anger under control. Acting on impulse would only lead to mistakes. "Think, think,

think," he said out loud. "Take your time, think, then plan your revenge."

Pacing the living room, it only took a few minutes for him to formulate a plan of action—a plan of retribution. Grabbing a newspaper from the recycling bin, he carefully pulled out the sports section by the upper corner. He hated sports and never read about them, but now that portion of the news was perfect for his plans since it wouldn't have his fingerprints or DNA on it. While his DNA wasn't on file, his finger-prints were. He retrieved a pair of scissors, glue, and a blank sheet of paper from his desk in the spare bedroom and placed them next to the sports section on the dining room table he rarely used. Finally, he pulled out a pair of rubber gloves from under the kitchen sink. He usually used them when he washed the dishes, but tonight they would keep his fingerprints off the note he planned on sending to that blonde-haired bimbo who called herself an investigative reporter.

He'd show her! He'd show them all!

Chapter 13

"I have a right to protect my sources," Jessica Daly told the two scowling men who were currently standing in front of her the morning after her big story broke on the evening news. "I'm not telling you where I got my information from. But it's obvious by your visit and the looks on your faces that my source was right on the money. If you're telling me some of my information is wrong, I'd be willing to correct it in my next broadcast. How about giving me an interview?"

She sat down at the table in the conference room she had brought them to for privacy. Making a show of crossing her shapely legs, she looked at both men expectantly.

Sean had been angry before he and Lynch had arrived at the Channel 4 news station, but now he was downright pissed. The reporter was actually flirting with them. Did she really think they'd be willing to give her a fucking interview? Not in this fucking lifetime, he said to himself, or the next. The woman was a leech, like most people in her profession. She didn't care how many victims were killed or how many families were devastated as long as the story was juicy enough to boost the ratings and her career.

"Not going to happen," Lynch responded. "And if you and your source are the cause of this guy getting away with murder, you'll be charged with obstruction of justice."

"It would never stick, and you know it," Jessica replied confidently. "Besides, the public deserves to know how sadistic this creep is."

Sean ran a hand down his face in frustration. They were getting nowhere with the reporter, but he could at least get a little revenge against her. He crossed his arms and glared at her with all his anger. "As of right now, your privileges at the press conferences regarding this case are revoked. I see you on Sheriff's Department property, and you'll be charged with trespassing. Understand?"

She sat up, her eyes flashing with fury and disbelief. "You can't do that!"

Brad looked at her squarely and smirked. "He can and just did. Consider this your first and final warning."

* * *

The two men stormed out as Jessica was still sputtering in disbelief. *How dare they?* Over her fucking, dead body was she handing this story over to anyone else. She would just have to find a way to stay ahead of everyone. Her sources would help, but she needed to do some more digging.

Still fuming, she returned to her desk just as the mailroom clerk left a thick stack of white and manila envelopes for her. Quickly sorting through her morning mail, she tossed aside most of the correspondence to open later. Three-quarters of the way through the pile, she stopped and stared at the stark, white envelope with childlike writing on it addressed to *Jessica Daly, Reporter—OPEN IMMEDIATELY—IMPORTANT*.

Jessica picked up the letter and dropped the rest of the mail on her desk. Turning the envelope over, she found no other writing, no return address, no mailing address, and no stamp. It had not come through the post office—someone had hand-delivered it. Taking her silver letter opener from the top drawer of the desk, she gently slid it under the flap of the envelope and sliced it open. It only contained one piece of paper, which she removed and unfolded.

The person who sent the letter obviously watched too many cop shows on TV. He or she had cut words from a newspaper and glued them to the page.

If you want the exclusive of a lifetime, come to 1279 Prescott Road in Elizabeth City at eleven o'clock tonight. Come alone and bring your video camera. I know who the Seaside Strangler is and have proof.

Holy shit! Breaking this case wide open for the cops and feds would get her on a national news team in a heartbeat. Pushing the rest of her mail aside, she opened up a new document on her computer and started typing the preliminary article. She'd add in the details later.

* * *

Sean's feet pounded the asphalt as he ran through the streets of Whisper. It had been just after three o'clock in the afternoon when he'd returned to the beach house and decided to get some exercise. He did his best thinking while running, and today he had a lot on his mind.

Suki had finished her profile and returned to Quantico at around 11:00 a.m. Sean and the detectives had followed up on a few leads from the tip line, which turned out to be dead ends. Before he left the station, he'd updated both Griffin and his SAC in Greenville. The story was now national news, and everyone was using Jessica Daly's moniker for the killer—*the Seaside Strangler*. God, he fucking hated the press.

As he jogged at a comfortable pace, his mind wandered to the night before. Following the newscast, he had been very subdued, his mind racing over the details of the case. They obviously had a huge leak at the sheriff's department, and he wondered how Jessica Daly's reporting of sensitive details of the crimes would affect the investigation. He was aware he could have been more hospitable to his guests, but the two women found many topics to discuss between them during dinner. He hoped their chatter had prevented his silence from becoming an issue.

After dinner with the two women, he'd held Grace's hand as they walked to her car, parked in the street in front of the cottage. As he opened the door to her tan Toyota Solara convertible for her, he apologized.

"Sorry, I wasn't good company tonight. That newscast threw me for a loop. It's really going to be a bloody mess at headquarters tomorrow."

Instead of climbing into her car, Grace stopped next to Sean and placed her hand on his chest in a comforting gesture. "Don't worry, I understand. Do you have any idea where the reporter's getting her information?"

Sean sighed and absentmindedly ran his hand up and down her arm. "It has to be someone in the sheriff's department, but that's Matt Griffin's problem. My problem is how the killer will react to all of this." He paused, then smiled. "But let's not talk about that now. You and Suki seemed to get along."

"We did," Grace said, her demeanor suddenly lighter at the subject change. "She's a lot of fun. I really like her." As she spoke, her hand caressed his chest in small, tantalizing motions, which heated his blood to a near boil—which then went straight to his cock.

"I'm glad to hear that," he murmured. His eyes left hers and zoomed in on her lush mouth. All thoughts of serial killers and coworkers immediately left his mind, only to be replaced by images of the erotic dream he'd had that morning.

Closing what little distance there was between them, Sean lowered his head and brushed his lips against hers. Sparks ignited, and he'd let out a deep groan as she kissed him back with a sensual urgency that caught him by surprise. She slid her hands up his chest to wrap around his neck as he silently urged her lips open with his tongue. Grace obliged, and he was instantly lost in the taste of her.

Sean took a step forward, compelling Grace to step back, and pinned her against the rear door of her car. He nibbled gently on her bottom lip before flicking his tongue over the same tender spot. From there, his lips moved along her jawline to the sensitive spot just below her left ear. She tilted her head back, allowing him better access for nuzzling her neck. He paused over the pulsating vein on the side of her throat and felt its tempo speed up as he made slow, lazy circles with his tongue over the spot. She gasped, and his cock grew under the zipper of his jeans.

As her hands moved up to tangle in his hair, his inched south down her sides until they reached her hips. Grinding his against hers, he wished they were somewhere they could get naked and do wild, naughty things to each other—things he'd been dreaming of since she'd first walked back into his life. He was just about to cup her buttocks and lift her, so her legs could wrap around his waist, when a car approached. Headlights illuminated them, and the driver honked his horn at them as he drove past. The sound startled them, and they jumped apart, panting from the experience that left them both wanting more.

Sean took several gulps of the cool night air and tried to bring his breathing and hard-on under control. "I guess that was the driver's way of saying 'get a room.'"

Grace chuckled as she tried to steady her own breathing. "Nothing like... making out... like a couple of teenagers... in the middle of the street, huh?"

"Actually, I can think of a lot better places to be making out." He waggled his eyebrows several times, making her laugh at his antics. Sean's heart skipped a beat. He'd just discovered there was no sound in the world more melodious than Grace Whitman's laugh.

Abruptly, he sobered. "Can we go out on a date?"

"A date?" Grace looked at him with surprise. "As in a date-date?"

"Yeah, a date-date. We've had dinner together four times, and never has it been a real date. So, can we?"

Sean stared at Grace nervously and wondered what he would do if she said no. He'd beg, that's what he'd do. For the first time in his life, he was ready to beg a woman for a date. Thankfully, he didn't have to. His heart skipped another beat when she gave him a shy smile and said, "I'd like that."

"So would I. How about tomorrow?" he blurted out, but his excitement disappeared as reality rudely intruded, and he grimaced. "Shit. I can't really make plans because of the case. I might be available tomorrow, and I might not. I'm not sure—"

Grace brought her fingers up to his mouth and silenced him. "It's okay. If you have to cancel, I'll understand."

Sean kissed her fingers before moving her hand away from his lips. "Hopefully, it won't come to that. I'll call you tomorrow around two. By then, I should have a better idea of what's going on. Is that okay?"

"It's fine." When he didn't respond, she added, "I swear. If you can't make it, there's always the weekend."

"Such an optimist." He smiled, dipped his head, and gave her a quick kiss on the lips before taking a step back to let her climb into her car. He knew if he did anything more than that, they'd end up really needing a room. "I'll talk to you tomorrow then."

"Great." She folded herself into the driver's seat. The convertible top was up due to a passing shower earlier. She pulled on her seatbelt and started her car as he reluctantly closed the door for her. He suddenly thought of something, tapped on the window, and gestured with his hand for her to roll it down.

"Do me a favor and call when you get home," he pleaded. "With this nutcase running around, I'd feel better knowing you were safe behind locked doors."

She nodded, said goodnight, and drove away. Sean watched the car's taillights until they were out of sight. He smiled and told himself moving back home was one of the best decisions he'd ever made.

Now, as he finished his run, he realized that not once during the five-mile trek had he thought about the case or that pain-in-the-ass reporter who had pissed the hell out of him this morning. Grace occupied his mind more than any other woman he'd ever known. And tonight they were going on a date. His body immediately reacted to the thought, and blood raced to his groin in anticipation.

Shit.

Maybe he should run another five miles and then take a fucking, cold shower. The sexual lust and energy which filled him every time he thought of her was driving him crazy. He didn't want to rush her into a physical relationship if she wasn't ready, but he hoped she was. He also knew, deep down in his heart and soul, that one night with Grace Whitman would never be enough.

Grace changed her clothes for the seventh time. She wanted to knock Sean's socks off, but nothing in her closet was exactly what she was looking for. She took off the burgundy skirt she was wearing and threw it onto the bed, adding to the growing pile of discarded outfits. A little meow caught her attention, and she looked over at the one-year-old cat lying on one of the bed pillows. Even though things now appeared to be moving in the right direction for Sean and her, Grace had kept her promise to herself earlier in the day.

After breakfast and running a few errands for her business, she'd gone to the local animal shelter and adopted a beautiful, velvety, grey feline. There had been so many cats and kittens to choose from, but this little guy had grabbed her heart when he immediately nuzzled up to her and then head-butted her hand. The staff told her his owner had died recently, and none of her family or friends could take him in, so they'd dropped him off at the shelter. Grace had changed that in an instant. A quick trip to the local pet store had garnered a litter box, carrying crate, scratching post, food, water bowl, and toys. An hour later, Grace's new little friend had been fed and was purring with contentment on her king-sized bed.

She reached over to scratch the animal's ears. "Get used to it, Rico. Your new mommy is a fashionista at heart."

She giggled as she thought of the night before. The look on Sean's face was so hopeful when he'd asked her out, Grace couldn't have turned him down even if she'd wanted to. And she definitely hadn't wanted to. When he'd said, "real date," her heart had skipped a few beats, and she couldn't believe what she'd heard. Sean Malone had asked her out on a date! She wished she still kept a diary like she did during her early teenage years. That very moment would have filled up at least ten pages.

Turning back to her closet, a flash of teal silk at the rear of the rack caught her eye. Perfect! She'd forgotten all about the dress. Her former coworker, Trish, had convinced her to buy the dress for a hospital Christmas party two years ago in New York. Trish had told her it was made for Grace's body and would drive men crazy. The just-above-the-knee length showed off her long legs, and cutouts bared her toned shoulders before the luxurious material flowed gently down her arms and torso. Grace had to admit Trish had been right—she'd definitely garnered quite a bit of male appreciation that night.

She held the dress up to her body and turned to

face the bed. "What do you think, Rico? Will he like this one?"

The animal continued to purr and flipped over on his back, paws in the air, tail swishing.

"You're absolutely right. It's drop-dead gorgeous. He'll love it."

Slipping the silken material over her head and down her body, she glanced into the full-length mirror on the back of the closet door and knew for certain this was the right dress. She finished off the outfit with a simple silver necklace, matching earrings, and the silver-toned high heels she'd originally bought with the dress. Her long, blonde hair was swept upward and softly held in place by a rhinestone clip. She spritzed a little of her favorite perfume on her exposed neck and wrists and took one last look in her mirror. Hopefully, she looked as good as she thought she did. If this outfit didn't bring Sean Malone to his knees, nothing would.

A knock on the door interrupted her assessment, and she glanced at the clock next to her bed. Six-thirty on the nose. Sean was on time, but Grace still needed to throw a few necessities into a small purse. Instead of keeping him waiting, she ran to the front door to let him in.

"Hi, I'm almost ready..." she said in a rush before her voice trailed off as she focused on him. He looked gorgeous standing there in a button-down, tan shirt, black trousers, and black dress shoes, spit-shined to a high gloss. He'd shaved and gotten his hair trimmed, but the lock of hair, which always fell just above his left eyebrow, was still there. She loved that lock of hair—it gave an impish look to his face. And, oh, his eyes—those mocha eyes were now wide with appreciation and a hint of something else—desire.

* * *

Sean's mouth went dry, and he struggled to swallow. He knew Grace was a beautiful woman, but—*holy fuck*—she was the sexiest woman he'd ever seen in that blue-green dress. He wished he had more than two eyes at that moment because he couldn't decide where to look first. Her legs went on for miles, ending in the sexiest high heels he'd ever seen on a woman. The shapely curves of her breasts and hips were perfect, and he was dying to taste the satiny skin of her exposed shoulders.

Suddenly, he didn't want to take her out to dinner, he just wanted to take her to bed. He didn't want any other man looking at her—he wanted that privilege all to himself. It was selfish, he knew, but he couldn't stop the feelings racing through his body, straight to his dick.

He didn't know how much time had passed before he found his voice. "Hi... wow... hi... um, wow..." Okay, he may have found his voice, but formulating a sentence seemed beyond his mouth's and brain's abilities at the moment. He cleared his throat and tried again. "You look beautiful."

"Thanks. You're looking very handsome yourself." Grace blushed under his continued scrutiny. If she had wanted to impress and seduce him, then she'd definitely succeeded. He wanted to have her for dinner instead of food. Inhaling deeply to get oxygen to his foggy brain, he entered the foyer when she stepped to the side to let him in.

Turning around, she hurried toward her bedroom. "I need a minute. I just have to grab my purse."

Sean closed the door behind him and stared at her retreating backside.

Holy shit! How the fuck was he supposed to get through dinner with a raging hard-on?

Tilting his head toward the ceiling, he breathed deeply and tried to get his body to behave. Something rubbed against his leg, and he glanced down to find a grey cat doing figure-eights around and through his legs. Sean smiled at the animal and squatted down to stroke its back. "Hey there, little guy. Who are you?"

"That's Rico." Grace returned with a silver clutch and a light, black cape in her hands.

"I didn't know you had a cat—he wasn't here when we had dinner the other night, was he?"

Grace chuckled as he stood again. "No. This is Rico's first day in his new home. I found him at the animal shelter this afternoon and fell in love with him. When I brought him home, he immediately strutted around like he was a king of the castle. No adjustments needed."

She handed Sean her cape and turned around so he could place it over her shoulders. He was disappointed the material covered up her bare skin. He opened the door for her while she bent down to scratch the top of Rico's head. "Now, you be a good boy, okay?"

Rico meowed his response, leaning into her touch. After one more ear scratch, she stood, then stepped over the threshold with Sean on her heels, shutting the door behind them. He placed his hand on her lower back, escorting her to his car, and she could feel the heat of her skin burning his hand even though the silk and light wool materials separated them. She shuddered as they reached the vehicle.

"Cold?" Sean asked. Without waiting for a reply, he opened the car door for her and took her hand to help her into the low seat. He silently groaned when the hem of her dress rose even higher as she settled in.

Heaven help him.

Chapter 14

The Elegant Swan was an upscale restaurant located in the heart of Kitty Hawk. Sean thought it would be nice to go somewhere new to both of them, and Brad had suggested it when Sean asked the older man for ideas. There was no way in hell he was asking his brother to recommend a place. He didn't want Brian to know they were out on a date —hell, Uncle Dan and Bonnie didn't even know. For now, he just wanted to keep Grace to himself, at least until he was sure things would work out between them. The last thing he wanted was for anyone else to make things awkward between them.

He held the door open and followed her through. The place was nearly full, and Sean was glad he'd made reservations as Brad had advised. The hostess greeted them and then led them past the bar into the rear dining room overlooking the ocean across the street. He didn't miss the appreciative looks Grace had gotten from several men along the way, and he placed his hand at her lower back, staking his claim.

After they were seated and their drink orders were taken, they both perused the menu. "The chateaubriand sounds delicious," he commented. "So do the lamb chops. What looks good to you?"

"The Chilean sea bass. I can't remember the last time I had that, and I love it."

The waitress returned with their drinks and took their meal orders. A busboy placed a basket of warm rolls and butter on the table before hurrying away again.

Grace took a sip of her wine, and Sean noticed she suddenly seemed as nervous as he was, but as he tried to think of a conversation starter, she beat him to it. "I... um... how was work today? Did you find out how that reporter got her information?"

"No," he answered, giving his head a small shake while he buttered a roll. "But at least I got a little revenge and banned her from all the future press conferences about the case."

She grinned. "Good for you. So what were you planning on doing these next few weeks if you hadn't gotten called to duty?"

Glad she was steering the conversation away from the murders, Sean swallowed a small bite of his roll. "Well, I was hoping to get caught up on a few books I've wanted to read, do a little fishing, and just relax.

It's been a while since I've had some serious time off."

"Fishing? Gee, I haven't done that since I was about twelve, and your uncle invited me along on one of your fishing trips."

Fishing was one of his fondest memories of Whisper as a kid and a teen. His father and Uncle Dan had taught the brothers how to fish as soon as they were old enough. There had been countless trips out on charter boats or just on the beach and piers to fish. It never mattered how much they caught, but there was always a money pool for the biggest fish reeled in. When they were young, it had been a dollar each, but now it ranged anywhere from $20 to $100, depending on everyone's mood.

"Well, then, we'll have to remedy that. Maybe I can take Saturday or Sunday off if there's nothing new with the case, and we can go fishing. That is if you want to."

"I'd love it. But you're going to have to teach me all over again. If memory serves me right, last time, I kept getting my line all tangled. Your poor uncle spent most of the day getting out the knots for me."

Sean chuckled as he finally started to relax. "No worries. After a few pointers, I'll have you tangle-free."

The rest of the evening went smoothly, and the conversation remained clear of the serial killer terrorizing the area. As Sean drove Grace back to her place, he wondered if she would invite him in. He wanted her in the worst way, but aside from the few steamy kisses they'd shared, he wasn't sure if she was ready for more than that. They'd gotten to know each other over the past week as adults, and he felt closer to her than any other woman he'd dated before. Maybe because of their history, but that had been so long ago, they'd almost started from scratch again.

Pulling into a space in front of her unit, he turned off the engine. Whether she was inviting him in or not, he was still walking her to the door. They both climbed out of the car and met on the walkway in front of her place. Holding Grace's hand in his, he strolled toward her condo. His thumb caressed her soft skin.

As they approached her door, Grace took her keys from her purse. "Would you... like to come in?"

Sean stopped and turned to face her. A heavy blush stained her cheeks, and he reached up to stroke her jawline with his fingers. "I would very much like to come in, but I'm not sure I could resist trying to get you into bed. I don't want to rush you, so it's probably best if I go home and take a cold shower."

"Or," her voice had become huskier, "we could take a *hot* shower together here, instead."

Gazing into her eyes, he searched for any uncertainty, but all he saw there was shyness and desire, the combination undoing him. He cupped her chin and gave her a brief kiss before taking her keys from her hand. Unlocking the door, he swung it open and then closed it again after trailing her inside.

Grace flipped a light switch, which turned on the two lamps in her living room, then tossed her purse on a side table. Before she could step away from him, Sean grabbed her around the waist and pulled her close. Her ass cradled his erection, and he couldn't resist thrusting his hips forward. She stretched her arms back and wrapped them around his head as he nibbled on her neck and exposed shoulder. Her perfume was sweet and sensual, driving him crazy.

A meow interrupted them, and Sean lifted his head to see Rico sitting on the back of the couch, staring at them. He shook his finger at the cat. "Sorry, Rico, but your first night here will not be in your mom's bed. I plan on spending the entire night getting to know every inch of her body. Now, if you'll excuse us..."

Giggling at his inane lecture to her new pet, Grace took his hand and led him to her bedroom, clearly intent on letting him do exactly what he'd just said. Sean shut the bedroom door in case Rico tried to follow them. When Grace's hands went to the zipper on the back of her dress, he stopped her. "Uh-uh. Let me."

She dropped her hands and watched him over her shoulder. Ever so slowly, he lowered the zipper, his mouth watering at each new inch of exposed skin.

When the zipper couldn't go any further, he peeled the dress off her shoulders and let it fall into a pool of silk at her feet. She was now standing in nothing but her black, lacy bra, thong panties, and her "come-fuck-me," high-heeled shoes. Yeah, those would stay on for a while because her legs looked gorgeous in them.

Pulling her against his chest and groin, he continued what he'd started out in the living room. His lips, tongue, and teeth, respectively, kissed, licked, and nibbled on her shoulders and neck as his hands reached around and cupped her breasts. Grace's head fell back onto his shoulder, and she moaned in pleasure. The sound went straight to his throbbing cock, and he ground his pelvis into her ass again.

Her hands went to his hips and held him in place as she gyrated her own. Unable to help himself, Sean bit down hard on the curve of her neck, then quickly licked the sting away. His fingers lifted the band of her bra, and her breasts dropped free. Spinning her around, he bent forward and drew one of her nipples into his mouth while rolling the other between his thumb and forefinger. He stepped forward, urging her back onto the bed. Before letting her lie down, he unhooked her bra and pulled it down her arms, tossing it to the side.

Shifting from side to side, Grace made her way to the middle of the bed, with Sean following, never leaving her breasts as he alternated between them with his mouth and fingers. He felt her trying to take off her heels and lifted his head. "Leave them on, Gracie. You look so sexy in them, I want you in nothing but them."

Grabbing the sides of her thong, he proved his

point by sliding it down her legs and throwing it atop her bra.

She removed the clip from her hair, letting it frame her face. Her gaze followed his hands as they undid the buttons of his shirt. His heart beat faster when she played with the rosy peaks of her breasts. Sean quickly removed the rest of his clothes and removed a condom from his wallet.

Shit! How long has this been in there?

His worry was gone in a flash as he remembered it was a replacement, after a colleague had begged for one after hooking up at a bar they occasionally went to for happy hour in Jacksonville.

Dropping to his knees beside the bed, he pulled her to the edge and placed her legs over his shoulders. One of the heels of her shoes scraped his back, and his dick grew even harder. He kissed his way up her inner thighs until his mouth found her bare pussy lips. He sucked on their plumpness, then impaled her with his tongue. Grace's hips bucked, but his hands held her in place as he feasted on her. The taste of her feminine spice was heaven. He could stay there and eat her for hours, but not tonight—there was so much more he wanted to do to her. First, he wanted her to come for him.

His fingers went to her clit and tortured the little bud as he fucked her with his tongue. Grace's breathing and moaning increased with each second that passed until she was begging for release. "P-please, Sean... I need... oh my God... please!"

The corners of his mouth ticked upward as he picked up the pace. Her orgasm hit her like a tidal wave. Her thighs clenched his head, her heels dug into his back, and her body shook with an intense force as she screamed her release. Rubbing her clit, he thrust the fingers of his other hand into her tight channel and prolonged her pleasure as best he could.

As she floated back to earth, she gasped for air. "Holy shit... that... that..."

Sean chuckled while reaching for the condom. "I'll take that as meaning I left you speechless, which does wonders for my ego. But the night has just begun. Move back on the bed, sweetheart. Let's see if I can get another one of those out of you."

Crawling onto the bed until he hovered over her, he took her mouth with his, and their tongues danced together. She sucked on his lips, and he realized she was enjoying the taste of herself on him. Her legs wrapped around his hips as he lined his cock up with the slit of her pussy. Her pelvis tilted, silently begging him to enter her. He eased in as her body yielded to him, and then he saw stars. Her wet heat drove him to near insanity, and he had to force himself not to rut her like a wild animal—at least not this first time.

With each thrust of his hips, he slid further into the tight channel until he was buried to the hilt. Grace's nails scratched his back, sending a shiver of ecstasy down his spine. He loved being clawed by a woman during sex. Why, he didn't know, but it was a huge, fucking turn-on for him. And tomorrow, he would revel in the marks she left on him.

Rising on his elbows, he pumped in and out of her while watching her expressions. Her eyes were open but glazed over as she bit her bottom lip. Her groans and gasps urged him on. Reaching down, he tucked his arm under her leg and bent it toward her chest, then shifted his hips to an angle that had them both moaning loudly. The woman was going to be the death of him. "Fuck, baby. You're so tight, I won't last much longer."

A tingling started at the base of his spine, and he leaned down, gently biting her nipple. As he'd hoped, it sent her flying again. Her walls spasmed around him, and white and black dots flashed before his eyes. Pounding into her, he felt his balls draw up tight and roared his release. Never in his life had he come so hard or so long. He shook with the impact until he was spent, and it took everything in him not to collapse his full weight onto Grace's body. Dropping his head to her shoulder, he struggled to get some much-needed oxygen to his lungs. "Damn... woman... and here I thought... it would be best... if I went home earlier... I hate to tell you this, but... I may never walk again... at least not until tomorrow... morning."

Beneath him, Grace purred like a kitten. "Well, you won't hear me complaining. Consider yourself invited to stay for the rest of the night, as long as we can do that again at some point."

Lifting his head, he smirked at her. "Oh, we will. Scouts honor."

"You were a Boy Scout?"

"Nope," he said as his smile widened, "but it sounded better than a pinkie swear."

Turning off the ignition of her BMW convertible, Jessica Daly stared at the decrepit tobacco factory on the outskirts of Elizabeth City. It had been shut down for nearly three decades after the company's cigarette manufacturing profits were eaten up by the larger, more popular brands. It seemed no one wanted to purchase the three-hundred-acre property and pay to have the one-million-square-foot building demolished —especially since there was really nothing else of value in the area.

Grabbing her oversized purse and the portable video camera she'd brought along, Jessica climbed from the vehicle, then shut and locked the door. It was a few minutes before 11:00 p.m., but the nearly full moon provided plenty of light. There was no other vehicle in sight, but several bay doors where trucks used to enter the building were missing, so someone could easily have driven inside.

To her right, a beam of light skittered across the

property toward her. Someone was signaling her from inside the building. Putting the straps of her purse and camera bag over her shoulder, she also made sure her gun was within reach at the small of her back—one could never be too careful. She'd gotten a pistol permit months ago after another street reporter in Virginia and her cameraman were shot and killed on live TV while conducting an interview.

Making her way across the cracked pavement peppered with weeds and garbage, Jessica scanned the area as she tried not to trip and fall. Thankfully, she'd worn comfortable clothes and shoes that were still appropriate for the camera.

A lone figure stood in an open doorway and pointed his flashlight at her feet. That was nice of him, giving her more light to see by. As she neared the doorway, she took in his appearance. He was a white male, probably in his mid to late thirties, and kind of cute. His brown hair was neatly trimmed, and he wore jeans and a blue button-down shirt.

He stepped forward and extended his right hand. "Hi, Ms. Daly. The name's George. Thanks for meeting me. I must admit, I wasn't quite sure you'd come."

Jessica gave him her thousand-watt smile. "And miss out on a great scoop like this, George? Never. Thanks for contacting me, and please call me Jessica."

The man blushed. "Okay, Jessica it is. Come on

inside. I have all the evidence you need to nail this bastard who's killing all those women."

Hesitating in the doorway, she surveyed the interior of the building. It appeared this had been a reception area of sorts but had more recently been used by kids having parties. There were empty beer cans and liquor bottles all over the place, and a couch had been brought in at some point for them to sit on. The stained and ripped fabric had her immediately deciding she wouldn't be using it at all. The walls were covered with graffiti and holes that looked like they'd been made by a combination of fists, bullets, and who knew what else.

George gestured to the other side of the large room. "Here, I brought a folding table, two chairs, and a camping lantern for us." After turning on the latter, which lit up the room, he switched off the flashlight and set it down on the table.

"Why are we meeting here? I mean, it is a bit out of the way. Why contact me instead of the police?" While she wasn't one to look a gift horse in the mouth, she was still curious. And that curiosity was what made her good at her job.

When she stepped over to the table and placed both bags on it, George shrugged, and his expression was one of embarrassment. "Well, truthfully, I didn't want to be known as the person who turned my brother in to the police. My family is quite close, and they stick together, even if it's the wrong thing to do.

They'd ostracize me if they found out I was the one who gave him up."

"Your brother is killing these women?" Holy shit, this was going to be an incredible story! Her mind flittered with how she would spin things in her newscast as she absentmindedly began to pull her pen, pad, and camera out of her bag. "Wow. That must be awful for you. How did you find out it was your brother?"

George didn't immediately answer her, and Jessica glanced up at him. Excruciating pain shot through her face as his fist made contact with her cheek, dropping her to the floor. Multi-colored lights flashed before her eyes, and bile burned her throat as she came close to vomiting from the shock. Her head spun, and he was on her before she had a chance to recover. She was vaguely aware of him tying her wrists together. Terror and agony coursed through her body, and she suddenly needed to urinate. Shivering, she tried to clear her mind and focus on what was happening.

Oh, God! What have you gotten yourself into? Scream! Do something!

But when she opened her mouth, a rag was shoved into it. He brought his face within inches of hers and snarled, "You think I'm a savage? A sadist? A fucking barbarian? Bitch, you have no fucking clue who you're dealing with. But you will—trust me, before you die, you'll know exactly who you're dealing with!"

Chapter 15

Arranging the bitch's body in the sand, George scanned the secluded stretch of beach again. It was at the edge of the Pea Island Natural Wildlife Refuge and didn't get the volume of traffic the rest of the shoreline did, especially in the cooler weather. But in a few hours, there would be morning anglers setting up their rods and chairs for some early morning surf fishing, so it shouldn't be long before his new victim was found.

Killing her had been such a high. She hadn't been like his usual tramps, and, for some reason, that had gotten him even more excited. Instead of carving "slut" into her torso, he'd given her the word that described her best—bitch. Her screams still echoed in his ears as he recalled stripping her naked and taking the knife to her skin. Her blood had been warm as it flowed from her body.

After she was permanently branded, he'd gotten to the part he loved the most. Taking a scarf, he'd wrapped it around her throat and cut off her windpipe until she'd stopped struggling and breathing. Then he'd performed mouth-to-mouth on her using a plastic shield to avoid any DNA transfer. Each time he revived her, he waited until she was alert enough to struggle again. He continued until he could no longer breathe life back into her and then let death have her.

He'd stepped back to admire his work and jacked off far enough away from her to, again, avoid leaving any of his DNA behind—not that it mattered since his DNA wasn't on file anywhere to connect it to him.

The earlier full moon was now dimmed by storm clouds passing to the west. He double-checked that at full tide, her body wouldn't get washed out to sea, then pulled out a penny from his pants pocket with a gloved hand. Placing it right above the bridge of her nose, between her open yet unseeing eyes, he completed his masterpiece. Like any artist, he took pride in his work. Maybe one day, after he was long gone from this earth, someone would associate his name with his work. He could give his lawyer a sealed envelope with instructions to open only after his death, but that was too big a risk. He'd have to give it more thought, so someday, the world could admire what a great man he was.

With one last appreciative inspection of his newest artwork, George trudged back to his nearby car. He needed to get a few hours of sleep before he had to report to work.

* * *

Rolling over, Sean grabbed his ringing phone from the nightstand in Grace's bedroom, silencing the ringer so it wouldn't wake her up. It was just after 6:00 a.m., and they'd had very little sleep last night—not that he was complaining. They'd taken that shower together sometime after midnight, then got all sweaty again around 4:00 a.m., which led to a second shower. Truthfully, it didn't surprise him that he wanted her again right now.

Tossing the bedcovers aside, he stood, pulled on his boxer briefs, and wandered to the living room. Rico passed him in the hallway, snubbing the man who'd kept him from his new mistress all night, and made a beeline for the now partially open bedroom door.

Sean's phone call had gone to voicemail, but instead of listening to it, he just hit the callback button. Matt Griffin's voice came on the line, and he didn't bother saying hello. "We've got another one. He dumped this one on the beach at the north property line of the Pea Island Refuge. I'm on my way, and so are Brad and the coroner. I'll call Brian and Rafe next."

"Shit." Sean ran a hand down his face in frustration, trying to bring his mind to full attention. "I'll be right behind you."

He disconnected the call as he returned to the

bedroom to find Grace sitting up in bed, rubbing the sleep from her eyes. Rico was by her legs, kneading the covers with his claws.

"What time is it?" Grace asked as she stretched her arms over her head. Sean groaned when the sheet she'd been holding fell down, exposing her naked body. And just like that, his morning wood was back. *Damn it.*

"Just after six." He held up his cell phone for her to see he'd been on it and searched for his pants as he tried to ignore the urge to dive on top of her for some quick relief. "Sheriff Griffin just called. I have to run."

"Oh no, does that mean there's been another murder?"

Zipping up his pants, he found his shirt. Thank God he always had a go-bag in the trunk of his car. He'd change into a clean T-shirt before heading to meet Matt. At least after taking two showers last night, he didn't need another one. He'd have to swing by the beach house for more professional clothing after he was done at the crime scene. "Yeah, but I don't know more than that."

Making sure he had his cell phone, gun, keys, and wallet, he bent over and kissed Grace on the lips. "I'll call you later. I'm not sure when, but I will."

He kissed her again. And again. Cupping her jaw in his hands, he deepened the kiss. Her lips were soft and warm, and he vividly remembered what she'd done with them a few hours ago. Of course, the body part of him that had also been involved was now hard as a fucking rock. "Shit. I want nothing more than to climb back into bed with you."

Another peck. A lick. A nibble.

Damn, if he didn't stop, he was never getting out of there. He was quickly becoming addicted to Ms. Grace Whitman and her delectable mouth.

Twenty minutes later, he parked next to a sheriff's department SUV and walked up a path between two large sand dunes. Griffin lifted a hand in greeting as he talked to someone on the phone, then pointed at a white sheet covering something in the sand about thirty feet away. Sean acknowledged him and made his way to what was most likely the dead body of some poor woman.

There were several uniformed deputies already on the scene. One was pounding wooden stakes into the beach to string up the yellow "Crime Scene – Do Not Cross" tape. Another deputy spoke to an ashen-faced, elderly gentleman with a fishing rod, a folding chair, and a tackle box at his feet. The guy had obviously caught something other than fish today.

Sean eyed the area around the white cotton sheet as he slowly approached. He didn't envy the crime scene techs, who hadn't arrived yet. They'd be sifting through the sand for a few hours with sieves to make sure no evidence had been buried under the ever-shifting grains.

Squatting, he took a deep breath and then lifted a corner of the sheet. *Fuck!* It was official. The bastard had struck again. And Suki had been right—this one was sooner than expected, based on his prior timelines. It took Sean a few moments to realize the dead blonde looked familiar, and then he realized where he'd seen her before. Dare County's victim number four was none other than Jessica Daly. Karma was definitely a bastard at times—the death of the aggressive reporter would be breaking news on every channel in the area.

Like the last victim, Jessica's stagnant, unseeing eyes were fixed on the clouds and seagulls overhead. A shiny 1993 penny was head up between her plucked eyebrows. Sean lifted the sheet more and was surprised to see the word "bitch" instead of "slut." The carved wounds had clotted long before the sheet was placed over her naked body, and the ligature marks on her neck and wrists were several ugly shades of purple, in sharp contrast to her pale, blue skin. Another prominent bruise discolored her left jaw and cheek, but nothing else immediately stood out to the seasoned agent.

"She must have ticked him off with her commentary the other night," Matt said from over Sean's shoulder. "She's the only one with that tag."

"If I were him, I would have been ticked too, but that doesn't mean she deserved this." He lowered the sheet again and stood. "Well, at least it answers our question about whether or not he was going to move on after three kills."

Voices had them both looking toward the dunes to

see Brian, Rafe, Detective Lynch, the coroner, and three crime-scene techs come single-file through the pass. The latter four each carried some equipment, duffels, or boxes. One of the techs immediately pulled out a video camera and began shooting the scene. When that was done, he would begin on the still photos.

The two detectives, Lynch, and Dr. Peter Hansen approached, and Sean saw his brother's eyebrows go up when he noticed the dress pants and shoes paired with a Baltimore Orioles T-shirt. Despite the gruesome scene, Brian was most likely going to give him shit over it, as he'd surely figured out Sean hadn't slept at home last night.

Hoping to head him off at the pass, Sean held his hand out to the coroner, who shook it and his head at the same time. "Agent Malone, I know none of this is your fault, but I'm starting to get sick of you already. No offense."

Sean's mouth ticked up in a wry grin. "None taken. I'm hoping the killer just made a mistake, though. He deviated from his norm."

"Really?" Hansen bent down, lifted the sheet, then whistled loudly. "Well, damn. Ms. Daly pissed in his cornflakes, now, didn't she? Who wants to take bets she didn't happen across our killer at a bar, club, or party?"

It had been a rhetorical question to which no one responded. He carefully and completely removed the sheet from the victim, then pulled out a thermometer from his equipment bag to insert into her liver for a body temperature reading. He'd use that in determining the time of death.

Around the group of detectives, the crime scene techs began their work with the utmost efficiency. After watching them for a moment, Sean pointed to where the uniformed deputy was still speaking to the fisherman. "Let's find out what he knows."

Rafe and Lynch stayed with the coroner and techs while Matt and Brian followed Sean across the sand. The FBI agent extended his hand to the witness. "Morning, sir. I'm Special Agent Sean Malone from the FBI."

The man nodded and shook the proffered hand. "I saw you on the news the other day, although I never thought I'd run into you out here. Name's Jeff Simmons."

After introducing his brother and the sheriff, Sean said, "I know you've already told the deputy here what happened this morning, Mr. Simmons, but I'd appreciate it if you went through it again."

"Sure. Although there's not much to tell. I'm retired, so I come out here to fish for a few hours three or four times a week. I'm usually here by 5:30 or 6:00 in the morning and gone by 10:00, give or take a half hour. It was about 5:40 when I got here today, and I actually didn't notice her over there at first—was chatting with my daughter on the phone before she went to work. I put my gear down here, hung up the phone, and that's when I saw a bunch of gulls swooping down." He shook his head in disbelief. "Thought I was hallucinating there for a minute. Got close enough to see she was a goner and called 9-1-1. My son is a detective up in Columbus, Ohio, so I knew not to disturb the scene."

"And we thank you for that—" Sean was cut off by the uniformed deputy, cursing and running toward the dunes. The other deputy was on his heels, and together, they prevented a news team from getting any further onto the beach. "How the fuck did they hear about this?"

Their witness denied making any calls to the press, and Sean was inclined to believe him because the man had referred to them as "fucking vultures."

Matt scowled. "My deputies and dispatch did this all by phone. Nothing went out over the airwaves per my orders. So they didn't get it from monitoring the police radio." Which meant their leak still needed to be plugged, or the coroner had one in his office now too. The third option they had to consider now, though, was that the killer had called them himself.

Running a hand down his face, Sean asked, "Matt, do you have any judges on speed dial?"

"Yeah, why?"

"We need a warrant for Daly's work desk and computer before her name gets leaked out. One for her home, too, but I want to hit her office before her bosses do."

The sheriff pulled out his phone again and scrolled through his contact list. "On it."

After Brian jotted down Mr. Simmons's contact information, he and Sean thanked the man, then started walking back to where Rafe was talking to the coroner. Two assistants had arrived with a stretcher to transport the victim back to the ME's office when the crime scene techs were done with the photographs and video.

Brian pointed to where the deputies had pushed the news team back behind the dunes. "They didn't get close enough for any shots, and none of us knew it was Daly until we got here, so we should be able to beat everyone to her office." When Sean just nodded in agreement, his brother clapped him on the shoulder. "So, how was Grace this morning when you left her bed?"

Sean stopped short and glared at him. "Really, asshole? Don't go fucking embarrassing her or blabbing about it—"

Holding up a hand, Brian cut him off. "Come on, you know me better than that. Busting your chops is one thing, but I would never do anything to hurt or embarrass Grace. Damn, bro. You've fallen hard, haven't you? You've never gone off on KC or me like that when we tease you about any other woman."

Taking a deep breath, Sean let it out slowly. "Yeah, well, no other woman has ever had me thinking long-term before. And shit, it's been just over a week since she showed up at the beach house, and I'm already thinking about asking her to move in with me. I've never wanted to live with a woman before." It was true. But one night in bed with little Gracie Whitman had told him what he'd already suspected—he would never get enough of her.

His brother grinned broadly. "And another Malone brother bites the dust. I just thank God it isn't me."

Chapter 16

Sean sat down at Jessica Daly's desk and shuffled through the piles of paperwork with gloved hands. Beside him, a computer forensics tech was packing up the reporter's hard drive to take back to the BCI office to look for evidence. Another tech had already picked the lock on a cabinet in the reporter's cubicle and had begun loading files into a cardboard evidence box. The sheriff's judicial contact had come through and issued the search warrant before the name of the killer's latest victim had leaked out. Daly's bosses weren't happy—seemingly less so about their employee's death than the fact the police were confiscating everything that might be relevant to solving her murder. Three men glared daggers at him from across the huge newsroom filled with cubicles, where they'd been herded out of the way by a uniformed deputy.

While the Malone brothers were at Daly's office, Lynch and Rafe had headed to her condo to execute a search there. Sheriff Griffin was currently at the ME's office. They all hoped that since the killer had deviated from his usual victim, he'd screwed up somewhere along the line.

Brian approached, carrying several evidence boxes. Whether the newspaper liked it or not, everything in and on Daly's desk and file cabinets was coming with them.

Tugging on the top kneehole drawer of the desk, Sean found it locked. "Anyone have a spare key?" he asked the men standing with the deputy.

When they said they didn't, Brian handed him a lockpick set that'd been in the inside pocket of his sports coat. Sean raised an eyebrow at him, and his brother shrugged. "Haven't met a reporter yet that doesn't keep their contacts under lock and key."

It had been a while since Sean had picked a lock, but this one was easy, and he had it open in under a minute. Pulling open the drawer, he saw the usual pens, paperclips, and other paraphernalia. Further back was a small stack of mail. Picking the stack up, he shuffled through the envelopes, pulling out the contents of each, trying to find a clue on how Daly had become the killer's latest victim. It wasn't until he reached the second-to-last envelope that he got excited. "Brian, look at this."

His brother whistled as he read the newspaper

lettering pasted onto the plain, white printer paper. "Sounds like we might have finally found a kill scene."

Sean grabbed one of the clear, empty evidence bags and placed the note and envelope inside it. He quickly jotted down the date, time, and location the letter had been found on the outside sticker of the bag. Standing, he instructed the techs and deputy to finish packing everything up, then headed for the door with Brian on his heels, ignoring the multitude of questions thrown at them from Daly's bosses.

Twenty minutes later, they were in Sean's vehicle on an industrial driveway, which was in desperate need of repair, and he grimaced every time he hit a pothole in his Mustang.

Next time we're taking Brian's truck, damn it!

The uneven drive took them about three-quarters of a mile through a thick grove of trees and shrubbery before opening up to a large expanse of property.

"Fuck!" Brian barked, and his brother's stomach plummeted at the sight that greeted them. There were over a dozen fire trucks, an ambulance, and three patrol cars already on the scene. Whatever the factory had looked like a few hours ago was long gone. In its place was little more than a huge pile of charred and smoldering ruins.

Just as they were about to pass a rotting sign with the former cigarette company's name on it, Sean slammed on the brakes, which earned a "What the fuck?" from Brian.

"Look." He pointed to the sign on the passenger side of the road. There was an 8" x 10" brown mailing envelope attached to it, with "Federal and Local Pigs" spelled out in large, cutout letters. Everyone else had probably been focused on the fire and missed it when they arrived.

Climbing out of the passenger seat, Brian pulled out his cell phone and took a few pictures of the sign for evidence, then donned a pair of disposable latex gloves he always carried in his sports coat. He retrieved the envelope and the two thumbtacks holding it to the sign and returned to the vehicle. Sean grabbed a clean evidence bag from his glove compartment and held it open for his brother to drop the tacks into. Not that they expected to learn anything from them, but you never knew when something would break a case wide open.

Brian then lifted the unglued flap of the envelope and slid out the contents. It was a piece of white printer paper similar to what had been used for the note they'd found in the reporter's desk. This one also had cutout newspaper letters spelling out the message.

I took care of the bitch reporter. Now back to the sluts. Someone has to rid them from society. S.S.

Flipping it over, the state trooper saw it was blank and sighed. "That's it? Well, the ME was right—Daly must have pissed in his cereal. 'S.S.,' I assume, is for Seaside Strangler. At least we know he likes the moniker Daly gave him. Let's go talk to the fire chief, although I doubt there's any evidence left."

Unfortunately, Brian was right. While there were sections of the huge building that hadn't been completely burned to the ground, there were no signs of a murder scene in them. An accelerant had been used, and the fire had been burning for a while, starting in the early morning hours, before someone had reported the smell of smoke two miles away. It had taken some time before the source had been discovered, as the sunrise finally made it possible to see the black and grey smoke rising from the building.

It was an hour after they'd arrived that Brian and Sean left the scene in the hands of the Arson and Crime Scene techs to sift through the debris for any evidence that might have miraculously survived the flames. And once again, they were back to square one.

Two Weeks Later...

While her new employee, Tim, ran an ultrasound wand over a patient's knee, Grace laid a moist heat wrap on another patient's shoulder before jotting down progress notes in their respective files. The small-business gods were smiling down on her. She had feared it would be weeks before they had more than ten patients, but Pro-Care had been open for over a week, and they already had over a dozen referrals from local doctors. At this rate, they would be running near full capacity in no time, and hopefully, within six months, she could hire a third therapist.

Up front, the new receptionist, Dana, greeted someone who had walked in the front door, but when Grace heard Sean's voice, she peered around the half-wall. It was still before noon, and she hadn't expected to see him until later. "Hey, come on back."

Her heart began to pound as he strode into the large room. They had spent almost every night together since their first official date, and each time she fell asleep in his arms, she'd fallen more in love with him. Sean Malone was everything she remembered and more. He was strong yet tender. Smart yet funny. Companionable yet dominant. And sexy as all fucking sin.

When they were in the same room together, the attraction between them seared the air. And between the sheets, it exploded. Yes, some might say it was fast, but in reality, they were old friends who had reunited—they had a past, as innocent as it had been. Now, she was looking forward to a future with him.

His smile didn't quite reach his eyes when he leaned down to give her a quick kiss hello, mindful of being in her place of business. She knew he was stressed with the murder case he was working on, and yesterday's discovery of another victim hadn't helped. This one had disappeared after leaving her job as a waitress in one of the local strip clubs two nights ago. Her body had been found near a dog park. Sean had spared her the details, but from what Grace had heard on the news and the haunted look in his eyes, she knew it was worse than she could imagine.

He kept his voice low so as not to be overheard. "Hi. Just had to get out of headquarters for a bit. My car kind of steered itself over here. Must have known how much I needed to see your pretty face."

Her giggle seemed to relax him somewhat. "Remind me to treat it to a premium oil change next time it's due."

"I'm sure my car will appreciate it." He leaned against the therapy table she used while updating the files. "I spoke to Suki earlier—she said to say hello."

"Did she have any new insight for you?"

Sean shook his head. "Other than she thinks he'll continue shortening his time between kills, no. We have another press conference this afternoon. I swear, since the reporter was killed, every major news channel from around the country has shown up. My office sent over two more agents, and the troopers have added a few more detectives. We've got hundreds of tips coming into the hotline, but aside from a handful of potential leads, they haven't been worth squat." He sighed heavily. "Then again, none of the potential leads panned out either."

Grace laid her hand on his forearm. "You'll catch him. I have faith in you."

"I just hope it's sooner rather than later. And now, to top everything else off, we have the politicians on our asses to solve this. As if we've been sitting around playing solitaire or something on our computers all day." He shifted his arm, so her hand slid into his. "Anyway, enough about that. How's business going?"

"Great. We had two more referrals today."

Tim must have caught his eye because Sean raised his hand in a brief greeting over Grace's shoulder before returning his attention to her. "That's fantastic. I think you'll do well here."

His hand went to one of her blonde curls and gave it a gentle tug. "Sweet and spicy... gorgeous and intelligent. It's a hell of a combination."

She gave him a suggestive grin and murmured, "You're just saying that to get in my bed again tonight."

The response she got was exactly what she was hoping for. His eyes brightened as they flashed to her breasts and back up to her face. He stared at her mouth as his tone became husky and as smooth as a fine whiskey, and the corners of his mouth tilted upward in a sexy smirk. "I kind of thought that was a given after the way you screamed my name last night. Poor Rico has a banshee for a mom now—at least when I'm making her come."

Thank goodness her back was to the others in the large room, and they were far enough away not to have overheard what had made her blush as desire coursed through her body. Grace didn't think she'd ever get enough of this man. "I seem to recall you shouting my name a few times, along with a hallelujah or two thrown in."

A bark of laughter escaped him, and Grace was happy to see him truly grin for the first time since he'd walked in. "Well, I guess my car was right. Seeing you was just what I needed. Do you think anyone would notice if we locked ourselves in the laundry closet and fucked like rabbits?"

"Um, yeah... I think we just established we are both loud regarding that activity."

"Ha!" He shook his head. "All right, it will have to wait until later. But be warned, sweetheart, it's going to be hot, sweaty, and dirty. Then we'll shower and do it all over again."

"Promises. Promises."

"Uh-uh. That's a guarantee." Sean gave her another kiss, this one lingering a little longer than the first, and it made her wish the day was over so they could finish what they both wanted to start. "I'll call you later when I have a better idea of what time I'll be off work. How does Chinese takeout sound for dinner? I'm not in the mood to clean dishes or cook... unless the cooking is in the bedroom."

She chuckled at his erotic leer. "Chinese and cooking in the bedroom sound perfect to me, lover boy."

* * *

Anger and frustration simmered in Sean's gut as he studied the pictures of the murdered women pinned on the wall of the training classroom on the lower level of the sheriff's department. Due to the increased personnel needed, they'd moved the task force into a bigger room.

Becky Travis. Shannon Emerson. Daphne Jones. Jessica Daly. And yesterday's victim, Whitney Wells. Five women. All were brutally murdered in the prime of their lives. Add in the three from Pennsylvania, and the bastard was rising within the ranks of some of the most prolific serial killers in recent history. The press was having a field day—every day—especially since one of their own bottom-feeders had become a victim.

The only thing they'd been able to solve out of this whole mess had been who'd been leaking the information to Daly before her murder. Deputy Larry Cumberland's cell phone number had appeared at least three times a week on the list of calls associated with the reporter's cell and work phones. The fucker had been leaking information to her and other reporters in exchange for sex and money. After Sheriff Griffin reamed Cumberland a new asshole, he'd stripped him of his badge and gun and suspended him pending formal charges being filed. Thirteen years on the job had gone up in smoke for a little extra cash and some nookie—Sean hoped the fucks and blowjobs had been worth it, but he doubted it.

Rafe and Brian walked into the room, drawing Sean's attention. He glanced at the clock and noticed there were only a few minutes until the press conference started.

"You sure about this?" Brian asked him.

Sean frowned but nodded. "Yeah. Daly pissed him off, and he veered from his norm. Suki thinks he may screw up if I piss him off. If you've got a better suggestion, let's hear it because I'm getting tired of spinning our wheels here. None of the tips has panned out. He's got no DNA on record, so the sample we got from under Daphne Jones's fingernails doesn't do us any good. Whether we antagonize him or not, it's a near certainty he's already planning his next homicide, so maybe we can shake him up enough that we can get a fucking clue as to who this bastard is."

Leaning against the table, Brian crossed his arms. "If you want, I'll do it." When his younger brother narrowed his eyes in confusion, he continued. "What happens if this guy decides to target you? You've got Grace to think about now. I'm not seeing anyone."

Since they'd celebrated Easter Sunday with KC, Moriah, Brian, Dan, and Bonnie, everyone knew about the couple's new relationship now and had all expressed their happiness over the union. It had gotten to the point where Sean couldn't remember what it was like not to have Grace's sunshine in his life. He was falling hard for her, and she'd told him the feeling was mutual.

Sean shook his head. He'd worried about making Grace a target but decided to take precautions to ensure her safety. He'd do everything he could to protect her. Still, if another woman were targeted specifically because of what Sean was about to do, he'd never forgive himself.

"No. I'll make sure Grace stays safe—I'll talk to her tonight. When she's working, Dan can keep an eye out from across the street, and she has Tim inside the clinic —I'll give him a heads-up too. And besides, it probably wouldn't matter whether you were seeing someone or not. All he's got to do is associate any woman with you —neighbor, friend, coworker. No. It'll also look odd if it doesn't come from the FBI."

A knock on the door jamb had them looking up. "Ready?" Matt asked, with Brad behind him.

Standing, Sean grabbed his carefully worded speech. "Yeah. I went over everything with Suki. She watched all of Daly's newscasts about the UNSUB and thinks what set him off was the name-calling. Barbarian, savage, and sadist were the words Daly used. Suki said I should use them and a few others."

"All right. Let's go piss off a psycho then."

They followed the sheriff down the hall toward the lobby. Along the way, Rafe cleared his throat as he walked next to Sean. "So, um, how was Suki when you spoke to her? Is she coming back to update the profile?"

Sean raised an eyebrow in curiosity and amusement. The other man definitely had a big-time crush on the good doctor. "She's fine. And, no, she has no plans to come here. She can update the profile from her office." He paused, then teased, "Want me to pass her a note from you at recess?"

"Fuck you, man," he grumbled in a low voice. "She's hot, and I liked the view. Nothing more."

Uh-huh. Like Sean believed that—not. But as they hit the front doors leading out to the press conference, his mind returned to professional mode.

The parking lot was teeming with reporters jockeying for the ideal spot to capture the news conference. CNN, MSNBC, and FOX News were there. Hell, even a news team from the BBC had shown up. Dare County's Seaside Strangler was now international news and fodder for true-crime fans.

Griffin took the podium first and released the name of the latest victim and some other information that was just a spin on what they'd released yesterday and the days before that. He then introduced FBI Special Agent Malone, and Sean stepped forward, placed his speech on the podium, and prepared to poke a rabid bear.

Chapter 17

Driving to work, George couldn't believe his luck. The karma gods must have been shining on him because the jogger who'd just passed him when he'd slowed while approaching a stop sign was none other than that fucking federal pig. He was certain of it after watching the news conference over and over last night, as his blood boiled with rage.

The fucking fed didn't get it—none of them did. The cops, reporters, and the friends and family of the whores he'd killed would never understand. Why couldn't they see he was making the world a better place by ridding it of worthless trash?

No, all they did was sit around and call him the same things that bitch had called him—a savage, a sadist, a barbarian. But this asshole had gone further—

calling him weak, a loser, dysfunctional, and, worst of all, a coward.

He'd show them he wasn't a coward—starting with the fed. Turning in the direction the bastard had gone, he knew exactly what he needed to do to prove his worth and get the pigs to see he meant business.

Sean's pulse and breathing were in their target range as his feet slapped against the pavement while he jogged through the streets of Whisper. Two miles down, two to go. He wished he hadn't unintentionally left his headphones and MP3 player at the sheriff's department yesterday. After he'd given his speech at the press conference, he'd needed to shut everyone else out for a bit. The music had relaxed him as he'd read through all the reports from interviews that had been generated from the tip line. It wasn't that he didn't trust everyone to know their jobs, but he'd been hoping that something that had been overlooked might jump out at him. It had been a fruitless effort.

Taking a random right, he alternated his route as usual. It was a way to remind him not to be complacent. Passing the empty playground of the local elementary school, his mind drifted from the case to the woman who'd rocked his world last night and, hell, the night before that too!

It was Saturday, so the therapy center was closed, and she'd gone with Bonnie to a yoga class this morning. He'd invited her to go for a run with him, but she'd confessed running bored her to tears. She preferred yoga, aerobics classes, and swimming to keep that sexy body toned to perfection, which he thought it was. However, Grace insisted she was too curvy. Instead of arguing with her, he'd kissed, licked, and nibbled every curve of her body last night to prove it to her. It'd been one of the best foreplay sessions he'd ever had, and by the time he'd entered her, they'd been so primed and ready that she'd exploded within minutes, taking him with her.

Checking his watch, he upped his pace as another vehicle passed him. Easter Sunday, earlier in the week, drifted back to him. It was the first time any of the Malone brothers had brought a significant other to the holiday celebration—KC and Moriah had met only a few weeks after the holiday last year. It had been his Aunt Annie's favorite holiday, next to Christmas, and in her memory, they'd always made a big deal about it. When the brothers were little, and their parents were still alive, the adults had a plastic Easter egg hunt on the beach with loose change and the occasional dollar bill. Even when they'd gotten too old for the hunt, the big dinners had continued. Now with KC and Moriah expecting, everyone was looking forward to starting the egg hunts for the next generation to enjoy.

An image of what his and Grace's children would look like, scampering around the beach, was interrupted by the sound of a revving engine. Some idiot was racing up the street behind him—in a 30 MPH zone, to boot. Glancing over his shoulder, he was about to wave at the driver to slow the fuck down when he saw the gray sedan was headed straight for him.

Without time to avoid the collision, Sean jumped and dove up on the vehicle's hood before it could knock his legs out from under him. The impact stole his breath, and pain shot through the right side of his body. He managed to tuck his head in, avoiding smashing it against the windshield as the vehicle's speed sent him flying back off. He landed on the asphalt with a thud that sounded like a sonic boom to his ears and rolled several times before coming to an agony-filled stop.

A screech of tires caught his attention, and he turned his head in time to see the sedan slow down and take a sharp right onto the next street. It was too far away and traveling too fast for him to note anything other than its color and that it was a four-door Toyota Camry. His vision was blurred from the impact and pain, so he hadn't been able to see the license plate or anything else that could be used to identify it.

"Oh, my God! Are you okay?" a woman yelled, her voice getting louder as she ran toward him. "Helen, call 9-1-1! Sir, where are you hurt?"

A middle-aged woman stood over him, and Sean

tried to focus on her face, but darkness overtook him, and he fell into a blank abyss.

* * *

Bonnie held her niece's hand as they waited for Sean to return from getting a CT scan. His dislocated left shoulder had been popped back into place, and a variety of X-rays were taken. The ER doctor didn't think he had anything worse than a mild concussion, but because he'd passed out before the deputies and medics had arrived, it was better to play it safe. The only other injuries were bruises along his left side and some road rash on his arms and legs.

Deputy Montgomery immediately recognized the federal agent upon arrival at the scene and notified Sheriff Griffin and Brian, who in turn had called his uncle. Dan had closed up the hardware store, then hurried over to get Bonnie and Grace out of their yoga class. After getting an update at the hospital, Dan called the oldest Malone brother and filled KC in. Thankfully, it looked like Sean would be released as long as the CT scan was normal. He'd be sore as hell, but it could have been so much worse.

Grace had never been so scared in her life than when Dan had broken the news to them. Not even bothering to change out of their workout clothes, she and Bonnie grabbed their bags from the locker room and followed Dan to the hospital. Although he was banged up and in pain, Sean was alive, and that's all that mattered to her. It had taken almost an hour for her heart rate to return to normal and the shivers of fear to dissipate. All she wanted to do now was take him home and nurse him back to health.

Griffin disconnected the cell phone call he'd been on and strode over to where Grace was waiting with Dan and Brian. "That was Brad and Rafe. There were only two witnesses—the woman who called 9-1-1 and the one who gave first aid. They'd been out for a walk and had just turned the corner onto that street seconds before Sean was hit. One of them is a volunteer with the local ambulance corps, so she knew what to do. They only confirmed what Sean told me earlier—it was a newer, gray Toyota Camry, four-door, with unknown North Carolina plates. They think it was a lone male driver but couldn't be positive. One thing they were sure of, though, was that the driver sped up and drove straight at Sean. It was intentional."

Running a frustrated hand through his hair, Brian cursed. "Shit. It had to be our killer. But how the hell did he know where Sean was? I freaking told him to let me do the press conference!"

Dan laid a hand on his nephew's forearm. "Easy, son. There's no point in being a Monday-morning quarterback. What's done is done. Thankfully, Sean will be okay."

"We've got an APB out on any gray Camrys with front-end damage," Griffin informed them. "We'll also get it out on the news. Obviously, this wasn't how we wanted it to go down, but maybe the sick bastard finally made a mistake."

The door leading from the waiting room to the ER opened, and the nurse who'd been treating Sean since his arrival by ambulance motioned to them. "He's back from the CT scan. As soon as we get the results, Doctor Romansky will release him as long as it's normal. You can come back and stay with him until then. He's asking for you all."

They found him sitting up on the hospital gurney wearing the fashion-less blue and white gown the nurses had put on him. The paramedics had needed to cut away his torn shirt at the scene to check for injuries. His jogging shorts were short enough to work around, so he'd still worn them upon arrival at the ER.

Brian had retrieved a spare T-shirt from the go-bag he kept in his vehicle, and now, he tossed it into his brother's lap. "Figured you could use that."

Grimacing, Sean pulled off the useless gown. "Thanks. Can I get out of here yet?"

"As soon as they get the test results," Grace told him as she picked up the T-shirt. Bunching up the fabric, she helped him put it on, sliding it up his left arm so he didn't have to move the injured shoulder more than necessary.

Between the two of them, they got him into the shirt, and then Grace leaned down to gingerly give him a brief kiss.

Lifting his good arm, he stroked her hair. "Thanks." He smiled. "For the help and the kiss."

"My pleasure." Her relief at his teasing was evident as she finally relaxed for the first time since she'd heard he was being taken to the hospital. "How do you feel?"

"Aside from getting hit by a car, I'm good—sore but good." He looked at Brian and the sheriff. "Any luck with the witnesses?"

Griffin shook his head. "No. They didn't have much to add to your report."

As he finished filling Sean in, the doctor returned. "Agent Malone, you're a very lucky man. The scan was normal, so I'll release you. Since there's no sign of a concussion, I think the reason you passed out was the pain from the dislocation. I'll give you a prescription for painkillers because I'm sure you'll need them when the Demerol wears off. Ice your shoulder on and off for the rest of the day. You'll be sore for a few days, but if it goes longer than that, I suggest you follow up with an orthopedist."

"I'm a physical therapist, Doctor," Grace said. "I'll take care of his shoulder and take him to an ortho if needed."

The man smiled broadly at her. "Perfect. I'll send the nurse back in with the discharge papers, and then you can get out of here."

"Those are the best words I've heard all day, Doc," Sean said. "Thanks."

Twenty minutes later, Sean carefully lowered himself into Grace's car, keeping his bad arm tucked into the sling the nurse had given him. Grace would take him back to her place to recover while Dan drove Bonnie home. Brian and Griffin said their goodbyes, then headed back to the Sheriff's Department to meet up with Montoya and Lynch to compare the rest of their notes. Brian assured his brother he would either call or stop by Grace's later to fill him in.

Starting the car, Grace backed out of the parking space and steered toward the exit. "We'll stop at the pharmacy on the way home."

"I don't need the prescription filled. I'll be fine," Sean sighed.

"Uh-uh. I can hear the pain in your voice, and it will only get worse when the Demerol wears off. You heard the doctor. Trust me—you'll thank me later."

Grace was happy he didn't argue with her. He could be a tough guy at work, but this was her field, and she knew he would be hurting later. And the last thing she wanted was to see him in agony when it could be eased with medication. *Stubborn man.*

Instead of staying in the car and letting her run into the pharmacy, Sean insisted on going in with her. While she stood in line waiting for his prescription to be filled, he found the over-the-counter pain meds and grabbed a box of Tylenol. Grace rolled her eyes when he handed it to her. "Fine, but I guarantee you you're going to want something stronger in about two hours."

"We'll see."

Stubborn, macho man! My incredibly sexy, stubborn, macho man.

Grace shook her head. "Why don't I run next door and order a pizza to take home? I only had a bagel for breakfast, and you have to be getting hungry. If you're not, I can reheat it later for you."

"I could eat some pizza," he agreed. "Go order, and I'll meet you in there when I'm done here."

Grace leaned in and gave him a swift kiss. "Don't you dare show up without the Vicodin, or I'll have a headache for all of next week if you get my drift."

She was half teasing and half serious. Starting tomorrow, she was going to do some physical therapy on his shoulder to help him heal faster, but the downside was that he would definitely be in pain without the narcotic. Sheriff Griffin had ordered him to stay home for a few days. They would keep him updated by phone, but they could survive without him for a bit.

"Yes, ma'am." He grinned and waggled his eyebrows at her. "You know, I like this take-charge Grace a lot. She's turning me on."

Chuckling, she sidestepped his subtle ass-grab attempt and lowered her voice so she wouldn't be overheard. "If I remember correctly, there isn't much that doesn't turn you on. But I'll be your Dominatrix if that's what it takes for you to obey the doctor's orders. Just don't make me get out my whip, little boy."

"Hmm," he murmured as he stared at her mouth. "Dominatrix, yes. Whip? I'll pass."

"Then you better do what I say," she ordered as she tried to control her smile and look stern. It was clear from his chuckling that she wasn't succeeding. "Get your meds and meet me next door."

"Yes, ma'am."

Chapter 18

By the time Sean's medicine was ready, he was willing to admit his shoulder was starting to throb. Actually, his entire body was feeling the effects of being hit by the car.

"Make sure you take this with food," the pharmacist instructed. "It can wreak havoc on your stomach. Do you have any questions about the drug?"

"No, thanks." Sean signed for the prescription and checked the box that said he didn't need a consultation before handing over the twenty dollars he'd had to borrow from Grace to cover the co-pay and the cost of the Tylenol. He'd only taken his house keys and weapon on his run, and Deputy Montgomery had secured the gun at the scene. It was then passed on to the sheriff, who had returned it to Sean when he'd been released from the ER.

"Okay, then, have a nice day," the man said with a smile.

Grumbling at the pharmacist's cheerful demeanor, he took the paper bag and headed next door to the pizzeria, where he found Grace paying for their dinner. His mood soured even more as he saw the man behind the counter checking Grace out. Dressed in her tight yoga pants, a body-hugging tank with a light-weight, zippered hoodie, she looked sexy as hell with her long, blonde hair pulled up into a twist at the back of her head. Of course, men would check her out, and this asshole wasn't the only one Sean had noticed eyeing his woman. The doctor, a hospital security guard, an EMT, the pharmacist, and a few other men had been ogling her with a combination of appreciation and lust between the ER and here—some subtly, others blatantly.

Jealousy was an emotion he hadn't felt in a long time, and it grated on his nerves. It wasn't Grace's fault she was a walking wet dream, and he'd have to keep reminding himself that men could look all they wanted, but it was Sean's bed she was sleeping in every night.

Possessively putting his good arm around her waist as she took the pizza box, he led her back to the car. Ten minutes later, they swung by the beach house, where Grace helped him pack a few clothes and toiletries so that he could stay at her place for the next few days. It wasn't like he wouldn't have been there anyway, but he'd been going back and forth to the cottage for his clothes.

As Grace drove toward her condo, Sean thought about their relationship. It was too soon to ask her to move in with him—hell, they'd only been dating a few weeks. But they'd been the best weeks of his adult life, despite the serial killer running around. He'd been in lust many times, but this thing with her was more. He knew it. He just wasn't sure if Grace knew it. Neither one of them had said the "L" word yet, but it had been on the tip of his tongue as he'd made sweet love to her last night. Was she ready to hear it? Was he ready to take that leap into commitment?

A wave of nausea came over him, and he swallowed hard. He was pretty sure it was from the narcotics in his body, combined with the aroma of the greasy pepperoni pizza sitting on his lap, and not from the "L" or "C" words bouncing around his mind.

"Are you okay?"

Grace's voice brought Sean out of the fog he'd been in—he could probably blame that on the narcotics, too, because he hadn't noticed they'd arrived and parked outside her condo. Grasping her hand, he brought it to his lips and kissed her knuckles. "Thank you for being there for me today."

"Of course! Did you think I wouldn't be?"

Shit. There was a hint of insult mixed in with her tone of disbelief. "No... I'm just... I like having you by my side. I'm falling for you, Grace. Big time. And it's unfamiliar territory for me. I don't want to rush you into anything, but for the first time in my life, I've found something... *someone* real. Someone who's taken my heart and given me hers in return." He chuckled and gave her a wry grin. "Please say you love me, too, before I start spouting poetry. If I did that, I think Brian and KC would demand I hand in my man card."

Leaning over the center console, Grace cupped his cheek and kissed him softly. As gentle as the kiss was, it still sent electricity straight to his groin.

Well, it's nice to know I'm not injured down there, and everything is working perfectly.

"I love you, too, Sean," she whispered against his lips. "No poetry needed."

He attempted to lift his arm to pull her closer, and sharp, hot pain shot through him. His sudden inhalation and gasp had Grace jumping back into the driver's seat. "Oh shit. I'm sorry, Sean."

"*Shh.* It's okay. My mistake." He tried to will the pain away, but the throbbing was getting worse. "But I think you were right. I'm going to need one of those painkillers. Especially since I plan on making love to you sometime this afternoon."

Shaking her head, Grace turned the engine off. "You're incorrigible."

"When it comes to you? Absolutely."

* * *

While he continued to work, George tried to keep his demeanor pleasant, so no one would notice how angry he was. Not only was the bastard fed alive, but he'd been released from the hospital. How the fuck had he escaped being seriously injured, at the very least? George had hit him doing close to fifty miles per hour.

The only good thing about the fed still being alive was George had found his next victim. The blonde who couldn't keep her hands off the bastard looked nicer than George's usual sluts, but in her skintight pants, she had men drooling all over her. And not just her boyfriend. Just like George's bitch of a mother, the blonde had no problem using her body to tease the opposite sex. She probably banged a new guy every week.

Well, he would put an end to that. After he was through with her, she wouldn't be teasing and tantalizing anyone. He could kill two birds with one stone, too—her wimpy boyfriend would be too bereaved to get on TV and insult George anymore. He'd pay— maybe not with his life, as originally intended, but George would definitely make the bastard pay.

* * *

Grace's heart soared. *He loves me! And I love him!* Once again, she regretted not keeping a diary because those announcements would take up ten, maybe twenty pages.

Sean was stretched out on her bed with Rico on the other side, grooming himself. She handed him a glass of water and a Vicodin, which he dutifully popped into his mouth. After he downed the medication with most of the water, she took the glass from him and set it on the nightstand. "Do you want to take a shower before that kicks in?"

Grinning, he took her hand and kissed it. "That sounds like an awesome idea. But I'll need help getting out of these clothes and someone to wash my back."

"*Someone,* huh?" Grace smirked. "Do you have anyone in mind?"

"Oh, yeah." He licked her palm. "She's a green-eyed blonde with a body that's a walking wet dream. She's sweet and funny and rocks my world. Know anyone who fits that description?"

Grace's other hand trailed down his sculpted torso to the waistband of his shorts. She pulled on the tied string, loosening it. "I might. You wouldn't happen to know if she makes you hard as granite, would you?"

His hips bucked as she tucked her hand beneath his shorts and found his growing erection. A moan of pleasure escaped him as she fondled him. Grace loved the velvety feel of him and how he responded to her touch. Sean bit his lip as she squeezed his shaft. "Oh, she definitely makes me hard—especially when she's naked in the shower with me. Think I could convince her to help me out?"

"Maybe." As she grabbed the waistline of his

shorts, he lifted his hips just enough for her to slide them down his legs. Her fingers caressed him as she ran them back up his leg, past his stiff cock, to the hem of his shirt. "Can you sit up?"

With her help, Sean sat on the edge of the bed. Grace carefully removed his shirt, trying not to jar his shoulder. Once he was completely naked, Sean spread his legs and settled her between them. "Now, take off your clothes."

"I thought I was a Dominatrix today. That means I give the orders."

Chuckling, Sean clutched her hips. "Do you take requests, Mistress Grace?"

"Requests, yes. Orders, no." Grace loved this playful side of Sean, despite the fact he was banged up and moderately high on painkillers. She was more than happy to take care of his needs—all of them—because she was so grateful he was alive. She'd thought she had lost him, and remembering how horrific that had felt sent a shiver down her spine.

Pushing away the awful memory, she stepped back and did a slow striptease for him. Through desire-filled and medicated, heavy eyelids, he watched her. His gaze roamed from her head to her toes and back again, heating her skin with lust. After discarding the last of her clothes, she turned around and sashayed to the bathroom. Over her shoulder, she ordered, "Stay there, lover boy, until I have the shower all ready for you."

One of the things she loved about her condo was

the updated master bath. It had a walk-in shower with a shelf just the right height to sit on. She usually used it when she shaved her legs, but today she had a different idea. She'd take care of her man—in more ways than one. Afterward, she'd climb into bed with him and listen to his heartbeat as he slept.

Once the water was flowing at the right temperature, she walked back into the bedroom to find Sean depositing Rico in the hall and shutting the door. When she raised an eyebrow at him, he shrugged his good shoulder. "While I love the little guy, I was getting creeped out by how he was eyeing my balls."

For the first time all day, Grace let out a laugh—a full-blown belly laugh. "I'm... I'm sorry. That's just the funniest thing I've heard in a long time."

Sean reached over and tickled her side, which had her shrieking as she tried to contain her laughter. "You think that's funny? Hmm. I think the Dominatrix is gone, and the jester has taken her place."

"Oh, no," she chastised him. "Mistress Grace is still here, lover boy. She's just enjoying some much-needed comic relief. Now get that cute butt of yours in the shower. Sit on the bench and let me clean you up."

Arching an eyebrow at her, he chuckled. "Cute butt?"

"Yes, cute butt."

"I'd prefer 'nice ass.'"

Grace lightly pinched the non-bruised side of said ass as Sean passed her on the way to the bathroom. He grasped her wrist and tugged her along. "No pinching my cute butt until I'm healed and can chase you around the bed."

Once they were in the shower, Sean did as he'd been told and sat on the tiled seat. Grace pulled the shower head down and began getting his skin wet enough for the soap. He hissed a few times when she passed the spray over the areas of road rash, but she wanted to clean them again in case the nurses had missed anything. His skin was raw and bruised, and again, she thought about how close she'd come to losing him.

Putting the shower head back on its hook, she grabbed her loofah sponge and the masculine body soap Sean had left in the shower because he didn't want to smell like her lilac-scented one. She gently sponged him clean, not missing a single inch of his body but being careful with the areas of shredded skin. His eyes followed her hands as they roamed over his sinewy limbs and torso. The tango had nothing on this seductive dance, which didn't require them to move their feet.

Grace saved the best for last. Foregoing the sponge, she lathered up her hands. When she wrapped them around his prominent erection, his head fell back against the tiled wall, and his eyes fluttered shut. She caressed his cock with one hand and fondled his balls with the other, taking her time. Sean bit his bottom lip as he brought his good hand up and covered the hand that was slowly pumping him. He didn't increase her pace, only the pressure, squeezing tighter.

"Fuck, woman. Who needs drugs when I have your hands and fingers sending me into orbit?"

Oh, but she was far from done. Releasing his heavy sac, she reached up for the shower head and rinsed him off. Going down on her knees, she reveled in the look on his face. His eyes were half-opened, and his nostrils flared as he anticipated what was coming next.

Lightly running her hands up his thighs, she asked, "Are you hurting too much for this?"

"Hell, no!" His cock twitched as if in agreement.

"Good," she responded seconds before her tongue licked him like an ice cream cone. She'd gone down on him before, but each time he'd stopped her before he came, wanting to come in her pussy instead. Today, she wasn't going to give him that option.

Before Sean, Grace had never been a big fan of blowjobs, but now, she liked giving them to him. Maybe it was his taste or because she loved him that made the difference. Either way, it didn't matter. She was just glad she liked giving something he so obviously enjoyed receiving.

Opening her mouth wide, she drew him in. Sean's head fell back against the tile again as he moaned loudly. His hand went into her wet hair and encouraged her to follow his desired pace. On the way down, she ran her tongue along the length of him, and on the way up, she sucked as hard as she could. His pre-cum salted her taste buds, and she craved more than the small sample.

Cupping his balls, she rolled them in time with her bobbing head. Sean's hand tightened and loosened in her hair at the same tempo. He slid down a little on the bench, giving her room to take more of him in. On the next down stroke, she went as far as she could go without gagging, then swallowed, closing her throat around the tip of him.

"Fuck! Oh, shit, please do that again!"

Grace was happy to oblige. When she lifted her head again, she tongued the 'V' just below the head of his cock. Her eyes met his when she released him. "Come in my mouth."

"Is that an order, Mistress Grace?"

"Damn straight, lover boy." She took him back in her mouth and increased the pace. Sean's hand tightened in her hair again, and she loved the erotic sensation that shot through her. She was horny as hell, but right now was all about Sean. Harder and faster, she bobbed her head, sucking and licking as she went.

"Oh, baby. I'm close. *Mmm*. Please, don't stop. Oh, God! Fuck, yes!"

Sean roared his release as multiple spurts of cum exploded into Grace's mouth. She swallowed as much as she could, but a lot seeped from her lips and rolled off her chin to the shower floor.

Panting, he reached over and wiped her mouth after she freed him. "Damn, woman... that was fucking... incredible. Please tell me... I don't have to get hit by a car again... to get a repeat of that sometime."

Grace kissed the inside of his thigh. "If you get hit by a car again, then you'll never get another one of those."

Chapter 19

"What the fuck, stud muffin?"

Sean shut the bedroom door behind him, so he wouldn't wake Grace. Suki had called the minute she'd heard what happened, and she wasn't happy.

"I told you to piss him off, not get run over by the guy."

"Trust me," he responded. "Getting run over was not in my playbook. But apparently, our UNSUB has a different one."

Suki huffed. "Apparently. Are you okay?"

"I'll live." He sat on the couch, ignoring the glare Rico was giving him from the recliner. The cat was still pissed off he'd been evicted from the master bedroom. "But despite my bruises and road rash, we're no closer to ID-ing this guy. Any new suggestions?"

"Yeah. Get eyes in the back of your head."

He snorted. The shrink loved to bust his chops, and he gladly took the comic relief. "I'll add it to my to-do list."

The doorbell rang, sending Rico scurrying down the hall to the spare bedroom. Sean stood and peeked through the front door's peephole. Sighing, he unlocked the door and opened it. "Suki, I'll call you back later. My oldest brother is here with his very pregnant wife... after I told them not to come."

"Don't blame me," KC told him as Sean disconnected the call. Moriah looked him up and down, evaluating the injuries not covered by his sweatpants. "When your pregnant and hormonal wife demands to see her brother-in-law, in the battered flesh, to reassure herself he's okay, you hop to it."

"I'm fine. See?" He did a 360-degree turn, keeping his injured arm tucked against his ribs. "I wasn't lying to you earlier."

"Stick it, both of you," Moriah chastised as Sean kissed her cheek while KC shut the front door. "Our baby only has two blood uncles, and he or she is not losing one of them to a deranged psycho if I have any say about it."

KC helped his wife sit in the recliner Rico had fled from. "Trust me. The baby is due in two days. If I could've convinced Moriah you were okay, we'd still be up in Little Creek."

Moriah waved her husband away. "Stop hovering. I'm pregnant, not a priceless antique."

"Well, not an antique, but definitely priceless."

Taking a seat on the couch, Sean watched his sister-in-law melt at the compliment before turning back to him. "Where's Grace?"

"Sleeping. We both passed out for a bit after we got home from the hospital."

"Oh, I'm sorry. We'll come back later." The woman struggled to stand again, hampered by her wide baby girth, and KC helped her up, rolling his eyes in exasperation. There was no way he would say his wife was driving him nuts, and knowing that, Sean bit back a chuckle. "We'll bring dinner."

Sean shook his head. As much as he loved his brother and Moriah, he didn't want everyone hanging out here later. At least if they met somewhere, he and Grace could leave whenever they wanted. "Why don't we meet you at Sassy's for dinner? Tell Brian, Bonnie, and Uncle Dan to meet us."

"Six o'clock?" KC asked while escorting Moriah to the door.

"Perfect." Sean held the door open for them. "The beach house is all yours, which you probably already knew since you came here. I assume Bonnie gave you this address."

"Actually, Dan did. He's already written you off as taken and headed for wedded bliss, by the way, so you might as well go engagement ring shopping because it's inevitable. That also means Brian is next in line for the old man's matchmaking. Can't wait to see that boy go down—hard."

Snorting, Sean had to agree. "That's going to be very, fucking entertaining. And I'm going to sit back, watch, and laugh my fucking ass off."

"So am I. Later, bro."

"Later."

Sean shut the front door and then ambled down the hallway to the master bedroom. Rico was sitting outside the closed door meowing, so Sean let the cat into the room and lowered his voice. "Fine. You can join us now. Just stay away from my balls, you little homo-cat. If you want a boyfriend, I'll get you one that's feline."

George pounded the steering wheel of his mother's car as he drove past the address he had for Special Agent Sean Malone. He'd switched vehicles and planned to hide his for a few weeks until he could get the damage fixed without raising any flags.

It'd been three days since he'd hit the bastard, and Malone still wasn't at the beach house. Finding out his address had been as easy as hitting a few computer keys. However, the night of the incident and the next morning, there was another guy and a pregnant woman at the house. No one had been there since, as far as

George could tell. The fucking bastard was probably staying with the blonde slut.

Doing a U-turn, he rethought his strategy. Maybe the sheriff's department would be the best place to find the fed again, then follow him. Yeah, that would work. But right now, George was itching to acquire a new whore to be turned into art. Something to tide him over until he could get his hands on the fed's girlfriend. But where to leave his new masterpiece? He pondered a few places as he drove past the beach house once again.

"That's it! That's how to lure that prick back into the open!" Formulating a plan, he steered toward home. Tomorrow he was off from work, so he'd have plenty of time to ensure everything was perfect. There were things to do and sluts to kill. The karma gods were shining brightly today!

"How does that feel?"

"Hmmm," Sean moaned. "Like heaven. But I think it needs to be lower, please."

Grace adjusted her hands on his back and shoulder. "There?"

"Uh-uh. Between my legs."

Chuckling, she continued to knead his injured muscles. "I know for a fact that area is working just fine. Besides, my first patients are due any moment, and I don't want anyone thinking a 'happy ending' is part of the therapy we offer here."

"Ha! No, definitely not." He reached back with his good arm and squeezed her ass. "That's a specialty for your lover boy only."

The front door of Pro-Care opened, and Sean released his grip as Tim walked in with two patients on his heels. It was a few minutes before 8:00 a.m., and after Grace finished the therapy on Sean's shoulder, he was heading back to work. Brian and the others had kept him up-to-date on the case, but he'd had to wait for clearance from an orthopedist, which he'd received late yesterday afternoon, to be officially back on the clock. Agency rules.

Tim helped an elderly male patient climb onto a therapy table. "How're you feeling, Sean?"

"Good. Got the best physical therapist there is working on me."

After finishing his massage, Grace retrieved a moist heating pad from the steamer and placed it on his shoulder. "Not that he's biased at all."

"No, not at all," Tim said with a chuckle.

Sean had filled the other therapist in on what had happened, so the guy knew to keep an eye on things at the clinic. With Tim here, Uncle Dan across the street, and a steady stream of patients throughout the day, Grace was as safe as she could be without being in a plastic, bulletproof bubble.

As she went to set up the other patient, Sean's cell

phone rang. Glancing at the number, he saw it was Brian's and answered. "Hey, bro."

"Where the fuck are you?"

Startled at the anger in his brother's voice, Sean responded, "I'm at Grace's PT clinic and almost done. Heading to the sheriff's department in a few. What's wrong?"

"Don't bother going to HQ. Meet me at the beach house as soon as you can."

He pulled the heating pad from his shoulder and stood. "The beach house? Why?"

"This sadistic bastard left you a fucking present. Victim number six—or nine if you count the ones in Pennsylvania—is on the patio."

Fuck!

Within minutes, Sean parked his Mustang behind a state BCI truck that had just pulled up to the curb in front of Uncle Dan's beach house. He rushed past the two techs gathering their equipment and ran up the driveway to the patio. His gut clenched when he saw the naked and mutilated victim perched on one of the outdoor loveseats surrounding a stone fire pit.

Shit!

He and Grace had been sitting on that exact piece of furniture after Easter Sunday dinner. KC had started a fire, and they'd all enjoyed sitting around it, waiting for their bellies to digest the huge meal Bonnie had served.

Behind him, one of the crime scene techs pulled

out a camera and began taking pictures for evidence. Sean looked at Brian, Matt, Brad, and Rafe, searching for answers that, obviously, none of them had.

His brother pointed at the house next door. "Mrs. Zielinski's nephew, Andre, is using her cottage for the week and spotted our vic when he came out to have his coffee on the porch. He went to bed around ten last night and didn't hear a thing." He lifted his chin toward the dead woman. "The killer left you a note."

What? Sean's gaze returned to the victim, and he pushed aside his anger that a place he loved and had lived in during his teenage years had been pulled into this mess. That was the least of their problems right now. The worst was the poor, unidentified, blonde woman who didn't deserve to die and be posed like a macabre Halloween display.

She'd been placed in a sitting position, but that didn't hide the word "slut" carved into her torso. The ligature marks were prominent on the pale blue skin of her neck, wrists, and ankles. She appeared to be in her early twenties and was similar to all the other victims with one exception—there was a white envelope on her lap with cutout letters spelling "Federal Pig."

Sean turned to the photographer. "Get pictures of the note so we can open it."

"Done. You're good to take it."

Brian handed his brother a pair of latex gloves. "It's your mail."

"Gee, thanks."

After donning the gloves, he picked up the envelope by its corner. "Does anyone have a knife?"

The second BCI tech reached into his open toolbox and retrieved a Leatherman multi-tool. "Here."

"Thanks." Sean opened the blade and slid it carefully under the sealed flap. He didn't disturb the glued area in case there was DNA evidence, but instead cut the top edge of the envelope to reveal its contents. Pulling out a folded piece of paper, he dropped the envelope into a clear evidence bag the tech held open for him. The others gathered around as he unfolded the single white standard sheet of printer paper. Again, the bastard had used cutout newspaper letters.

Hope you enjoy your get-well present. Next time you won't be so lucky. S.S.

With sarcasm dripping from every word, Sean said, "*Aw*, and here I thought he didn't care. Son of a bitch." He resisted the irrational urge to crumple the paper up and placed it in another evidence bag the tech handed him.

The ME and two attendants stepped onto the patio, and Dr. Hansen shook his head. "This guy is really starting to piss me off, Sheriff."

Crossing his arms, Matt grunted. "I'm way past 'starting to' get pissed off. Can BCI take some fingerprints before you take her? I want to find out who she is as fast as possible."

Hansen nodded at one of the attendants. "Make sure you scrape under her nails before doing the prints."

As everyone did their jobs, Brian stepped over to Sean and lowered his voice. "Rock, paper, scissors?"

"For what?"

"Winner sits in on the autopsy. Loser tells Uncle Dan his beloved beach house is now a homicide crime scene."

Fuck.

Chapter 20

Grace waved goodbye to Elsie Whitmore as Tim finished up with Mr. Berkeley. The day had been filled with a steady stream of clients needing rehab. She hadn't expected the patient volume to rise quickly and was already considering hiring another physical therapist for part-time hours.

Glancing at the clock, she wondered if Sean was running late. He'd hoped to be there at six when she closed, and then he'd follow her home. If he wasn't on time, she would walk across the street to Dan's apartment above the hardware shop until he arrived. She thought he was being overprotective, but this was his field, and after he'd gotten hit by the car, she understood his caution.

Sean returned after informing Dan about the crime scene at the beach house. Grace felt bad because she knew how much the little cottage meant to the older man. And now it was sullied because of a madman, and no amount of good memories would erase the fact that a woman had been brutally murdered and left there.

Sean had filled her in as much as he could, and her heart broke at his frustration. There were evil people in the world, and being in the FBI, he'd come across many of them, she was sure. But this case was eating at him, and she prayed they got a break soon so the task force and the residents of Dare County could breathe easier again.

Gathering up the top of a plastic garbage bag, she pulled it out of the can it was in and looked around to see if anything else needed to be thrown away. Tim was doing an ultrasound treatment on Mr. Berkeley, which would last several minutes, so Grace started for the back door leading to the alley, where the employees working in the few stores on either side of her were parked. Most of them would be gone by this time, but a few would still be there. The dumpster for the businesses in her complex was back there.

Opening the door, she made sure it didn't shut completely behind her and locked herself out by putting a small wedge between it and the door jamb. The dumpster was two stores down to her right, and Grace swung the garbage bag as a silly tune popped into her head. Maybe she would find a comedy on Netflix tonight for Sean—after the day he had, he could probably use some comic relief.

When she reached the dumpster, she lifted the lid, threw the bag inside, then let the lid drop again. Before she could turn around, two arms encircled her from behind. One hand grabbed her waist while the other clamped a cloth over her mouth and nose. A sickeningly sweet smell filled her nostrils as she reached up and tried to pull the cloth away from her face, clawing at the hand holding it.

Grace struggled against the assault, kicking and trying to break free, but her mind began to fog, and the strength drained from her limbs, rendering them useless. As she gave one last, futile kick of her leg, her slip-on sneaker flew from her foot. Her body went limp as heavy darkness overtook her. The last thing she heard before she lost consciousness was a male voice say, "Sleep tight... slut."

Parking the Mustang in an empty spot in front of Grace's business, Sean glanced at his watch—6:02. Not bad. With the horrendous day behind him, he was looking forward to cuddling on the couch with the woman he loved, some takeout, a funny movie or show, and Rico purring loudly in the middle of it all. When the cat wasn't being moody, he loved to lie on the back of the couch behind them and purr in their ears.

Sean climbed out of his car just as Dan locked up the hardware store. The older man held up a finger, and Sean waited for him to cross the street with Jinx at his side. Tail wagging, the dog sniffed Sean earnestly, probably smelling Rico on his clothes.

"How was the rest of your day?" Dan asked.

Leaning against the hood of the car, Sean crossed his arms. The weight of his frustration and anger was apparent on his face. "It sucked. This morning's victim was the niece of Congressman Holloway, Natalie Bowers. She went to a bachelorette party at a club in Elizabeth City last night and never made it home. Her friends said she met them there, and they didn't see her leave with anyone, but the place was packed. She left early—around 11:00 p.m.—because she was supposed to run in some 5k fundraiser for veterans today, but her car was found in the club's lot this morning.

"The ME estimated the time of death was sometime between midnight and two a.m. Her prints were in the system from when her father was a US ambassador to Belgium while she was in her teens. Her parents are on vacation in Hawaii, so her name won't be released until the morning, while they fly back tonight. The congressman notified them by phone a few hours ago."

He shrugged his bad shoulder and grimaced. It had felt better most of the day, but now his neck was stiff with stress, and that was affecting the still-healing muscles. Grace planned to massage it again tonight, then put a heating pad on it. "Anyway, let's talk about something else. How was your day?"

"Good. Bonnie and I are going out to eat and then to see that new movie we were talking about the other night. Want to join us?"

He shook his head. "No, thanks. I just want to go home, kick off my shoes, and order takeout. I'd probably be asleep ten minutes into a movie."

"I hear ya. So..." Sean's brow furrowed when his uncle's words trailed off. The man was grinning, with a twinkle in his eye.

"What?"

Dan shrugged not-so-innocently. "Nothing. Just wondering how things are going for you and Grace."

"Oh, no." Sean shook a finger at him. "Don't start. At least, let me close this case before you and Bonnie start planning our wedding. Speaking of which, you two have been spending a lot of time together lately. More so than usual." He arched a questioning eyebrow. "Something you want to tell the rest of us?"

The man's smile got even wider. Oh, yeah, something was definitely going on. "Well, since you asked, I've started courting Bonnie."

A laugh burst from Sean's chest—the first one since he'd been joking around with Grace that morning. "Courting? Do people still do that nowadays?"

"I don't care what other people call it or do nowadays. I courted Annie, although it didn't last long. We were married two months after we met."

Sean knew that story well, but he couldn't imagine going from just meeting someone to wedded bliss eight weeks later—even though that was basically what KC and Moriah had done, give or take a week.

Apparently, back in the day, it wasn't unheard of at all. In fact, his parents had only been "courting" three and a half months before they got engaged. But unlike Dan and Annie's elopement, Tom and Megan Malone had done the church-and-reception thing after a six-month engagement. "Well, good for you. I'm happy for both of you. But why now, after all this time? Annie's been gone for almost thirty years, and you and Bonnie have been good friends all along."

This time, Dan shrugged. "I don't know, to tell you the truth. Things just changed for the better between us, and I guess the time was right."

"So when's the wedding?" Sean teased.

"Don't you turn the tables on me, boy. I'm getting all three of you married off before I can relax and settle down. You're not getting any younger, you know."

"That's calling the kettle black, old man." He pushed off the car and clapped his uncle on the back. "Anyway, you and Bonnie have fun. Let me go get Grace and find out what she wants for dinner tonight."

"I'm right behind you. She called a little while ago and asked me to bring over a wrench after I closed." He pulled the tool out of his back pocket. "The hose for the washing machine is dripping a little."

Sean pulled open the door to the business, and Jinx rushed past him, looking for one of his favorite humans.

Grace's receptionist had left at the end of her shift at 4:00 p.m., so no one was sitting at the front desk.

The two men entered the large therapy room, and Sean glanced around. The only people there were Tim and an older gentleman who was buttoning up his dress shirt and getting ready to leave.

As Dan headed toward the laundry room, Sean asked Tim, "Where's Grace?"

The man pointed toward the back door. "She took the garbage out." He checked the clock as if suddenly realizing more time had passed than he thought. "But that was about ten minutes ago."

Panicking, Sean set off at a dead run and slammed into the back door, throwing it wide open. His gaze went everywhere, hoping to find Grace was just talking to someone, having lost track of time.

Jinx followed on his heels, and he heard Dan and Tim also come out behind him. Grace was nowhere in sight, and her car was still parked in a space in the small lot.

"Grace!" he shouted, then pointed for Dan to head left while he went right and for Tim to check the car. "Grace!"

Jinx made a beeline to the dumpster two stores down, sniffing like mad, seemingly understanding the situation's urgency. The dog was the first one to spot the single, white, slip-on shoe Grace had been wearing earlier, and Sean's heart and stomach sank when he saw it. Jinx sniffed the shoe, then whined and looked up at him in confusion.

Leaving the shoe where it was, Sean pulled out his cell phone and found the number for the direct line to the on-duty desk sergeant at the sheriff's department.

Fuck! Please let this be a nightmare or a joke. Please!

When the call was answered, he spoke with authority and a calm he didn't feel. "This is Special Agent Sean Malone of the FBI. I need the sheriff and BCI to respond immediately to 113 Main Street in Whisper for a kidnapping by an unknown suspect. Grace Whitman, blonde female Caucasian, twenty-seven, last seen wearing khaki pants and a navy blue polo shirt. Abduction took place in the last ten to fifteen minutes. No description of a vehicle or suspect. Also, contact Detective Brad Lynch and have him respond."

After the sergeant confirmed the information, Sean disconnected the phone and turned to find his uncle looking pale and terrified. It was exactly how Sean felt. "Go be with Bonnie. I'll call you as soon as I know anything."

His uncle gave him a stoic nod. "Let me know if you need anything. I'll be praying for you both."

"So will I."

I'm going to pray as if the love of my life's life depends on it. Because it does.

* * *

Pulling the car into the detached garage of his aunt's home, George got out and shut the overhead door, blocking any view the neighbors might have. He hadn't known his mother's sister had ever existed until he was contacted by her lawyer after she'd passed away. The woman had never married and had no children, but her life had been far better than her sibling's.

After years of disappointing her family left and right with poor decisions, George's mother had run away from home at seventeen because she believed her boyfriend loved her more than her parents had. That dirtbag had apparently been George's sperm donor and had abandoned his girlfriend faster than he could take a dump when he found out she was pregnant.

Instead of returning to her prim and proper family for help, George's mother had gone on welfare and worked her way through a steady stream of johns and boyfriends. Luckily for her son, she hadn't been into the heavy drugs of heroin and crack until a year or so after he was born.

Whereas his mother had always been a whiny bitch who hadn't given a crap about anyone but herself, her sister had been a successful businesswoman with a nice suburban home and an even nicer bank account. How she knew about George and why she hadn't tried to find him before her death was a mystery that she took to her grave. All her lawyer had was George's name, date of birth, and an address in Philadelphia, where George and his mother had lived when he'd been in elementary school.

His aunt had left instructions to hire a private investigator to find her only living heir upon her death. While part of him had been thrilled at his windfall, the other part hated the woman for not rescuing him from his crappy childhood.

Opening the trunk, he reached in and lifted the unconscious woman, carrying her up the stairs to the second floor. The large, windowless room had been the first thing he'd renovated in the house. He'd tripled the insulation in the walls, ceiling, and floor, making it soundproof. It was now the place where the women he abducted became his masterpieces. No matter how much they screamed while he carved them, no one heard them but him—it was music to his ears. This was his playroom. The only one he hadn't killed in this room since moving from Pennsylvania had been the bitch reporter. He hadn't wanted to risk her telling anyone she was meeting him for the "exclusive," and she didn't deserve to be brought here after the names she'd called him.

The only thing that was still bothering him about this latest snatch was the cameras he'd seen at the firehouse after he'd driven by with his prize in the trunk. A reporter had been talking with some firemen in front of the station. It shouldn't be a problem, though, because several cars had been on the street then, and he was just another person heading home from work or going out to meet some friends.

He dropped the slut unceremoniously onto a plank table in the middle of the room. She would wake up soon, and he quickly restrained her wrists and ankles.

As he finished securing her, his cell phone chirped. One of the other things he'd added to the house was a security system that he could control via his smartphone or computer. The alert was for someone ringing the bell at the front door of the house.

Bringing up the picture of whoever was interrupting him, he rolled his eyes when an elderly neighbor from across the street appeared.

Fucking pain in the ass.

Every time she spotted him arriving at the house, she came over with some request for him to help her out—usually with something that needed to be repaired at her place. Whomever she'd bugged before him was probably thrilled she'd found someone else to annoy. Maintaining his friendly persona around her was getting harder every fucking day. He should just kill the bitch and end his misery.

The alert sounded again. The irritating woman would continue pressing it until he answered the door —she must wait at her front window, just watching for him to pull into the drive.

Not worried about the slut screaming, he locked the door behind him and hurried down the stairs. Putting on his "nice neighbor" smile, he exited the garage through the pedestrian door and walked down the driveway instead of going through the house. "Mrs. Pennington? I'm over here."

Turning away from the door where she'd been about to press the bell again, she looked at him in relief. "Oh, George. There you are. I hope I'm not bothering you."

He fought the urge to roll his eyes or punch her in the face. "Well, I was kind of in the middle of something..."

Letting his voice trail off, he hoped she would get the picture. No such luck.

"Oh, I'm sorry, but I was hoping you could just help me for a moment. My hallway light is out, and I'm too old to climb up on a chair to change it. That, and I think I'm too short, even with the chair," she added with a chuckle.

His laughter at her lame joke was forced and didn't reach his eyes. He wanted her four-eyed, wrinkled face gone from his sight, but he'd worked hard to make the neighbors in the area think he was just a nice, quiet guy. He even had some of them bring him dinner and baked goods. Meanwhile, a few had tried to set him up with their daughters, granddaughters, nieces, or friends, which he'd gotten out of by conjuring up a long-distance relationship. The last thing he needed was anyone thinking he was rude or that something nefarious was going on behind his closed doors, and he still had some time before the slut woke up. "Sure, Mrs. Pennington. I'd be happy to help."

Chapter 21

Everyone had swarmed to the scene as Sean's panic and anger raged. He should have known... *fuck!* He should have fucking known the bastard would come after him again, and what better way than to take the woman he loved? But how the fuck had the killer known about Grace? Sean had been careful about being followed. He'd had one of the deputies check under his car a few minutes ago for a tracking device—nothing.

"Fuck!"

Brian startled next to him. "What?"

"This morning was a setup. It was more than him telling me he knew where I lived. My mind was all over the place as I drove back over here, trying to think of how to tell Dan the house was a crime scene." He ran a hand through his hair, fighting the urge to punch the brick wall of the building behind him. "Honestly, I don't even remember the drive—the bastard could have been right on my ass, and I was so distracted I wouldn't have even known it. This is my fucking fault! All of it!"

"Hey!" Brian grabbed him by the shoulders and got in his face. "This is not your fault, brother. It's that fucking, psychotic asshole's fault. Now, settle down, and let's think this through. Pull it the fuck together."

As much as he didn't believe Brian, Sean knew his last statement was what was needed. He could deal with the guilt of Grace's kidnapping after they found her—alive and unharmed. "All right. All right."

He glanced around. The deputies were questioning everyone they could find at businesses and in homes within a three-block radius. The BCI techs were taking pictures and checking the dumpster and Grace's car for any possible evidence. There were no fucking cameras in the alley, and none of the small shops on either side of the street had security cameras outside, so they couldn't even look for pictures of a car driving past or out of the alley. That was one of the drawbacks of small towns with very little crime.

"Got something!"

The two brothers turned, and Griffin and Lynch joined them as Rafe came jogging down the alley from the opposite direction of the dumpster. A TV camera crew was running behind him while an older gentleman was shuffling along, trying to keep up with everyone.

What the fuck?

Sean was just about to yell at the media sharks, but Rafe held up a hand to stop him. "We think we might have him on camera. Mr. Tomkins lives down the side street. He was walking his dog and said he saw a man sitting in a white sedan at the end of the parking lot, but he didn't think anything of it. Figured the guy was picking up a wife or girlfriend getting off of work."

"I'm sorry I didn't question him," Mr. Tomkins said.

"It's all right, sir," Rafe assured the man before turning back to the others. "The camera crew was filming some footage at the firehouse, two blocks down, for the fundraiser they're having next week. They were facing down the street toward Grace's place, getting the firehouse, park, and businesses in the shot."

Sean finally got it. "So we may have the guy driving past?"

"Yup."

One of the two men from the news team held up a laptop so everyone could see and hit a button that started the video on the screen. "We get an exclusive out of this, right?" His face fell when all five lawmen glared at him with the threat of impending death. "Can't blame me for trying."

The video began inside the firehouse garage, and the guy hit a button, fast-forwarding the footage before stopping it. "This is the start of where the camera is pointing down the street."

Rafe stepped to the side so Mr. Tomkins could get

a better view. One minute passed. Two minutes. Several cars appeared on the screen and then disappeared again. The sound was muted, so all they had was the video. Beside Sean, Brian tensed, and he knew his brother had seen what he'd also spotted. In the distance, a white car had pulled out onto the street, heading toward the camera. From that far away, it could have come from the driveway leading toward the rear parking lot they were now standing in, but they needed the witness to ID it without any coaching.

"That's it!" Tomkins exclaimed. "That sure as hell looks like it."

That was good enough for them to put out an APB on the car, but they couldn't make out the driver or the license plate on the small screen. Sean held out his hand to the guy holding the laptop. "Let me have the disk. We need to get it to the lab to clear up the driver's face to see if we can ID him."

The cameraman shook his head. "No need. I've got a setup in the van that's pretty advanced. I can probably have it for you in about ten minutes."

Everyone looked at Sean. Not only was he the lead federal agent on the scene, but it was his woman in peril. He nodded his head once. "Do it."

After the cameraman ran back to the firehouse and drove the news van closer to the scene, Sean climbed into the back with him while everyone else waited outside the sliding side door. There was scarcely enough room for Sean to be in there, and twice he'd banged his still tender shoulder on a low cabinet that hung behind the passenger seat. He was barely holding it together and fought the urge to yell at the guy to hurry up.

Working as fast as he could, the cameraman typed on the keyboard, moved a mouse, turned dials, and flipped switches on a control board. Soon, he had the image on the screen and began adjusting the pixels. An attempt to read the license plate failed, as it had been smeared with mud or something similar.

"Shit. Try the driver," Sean instructed.

As the picture zoomed in on the driver and slowly became clearer, something niggled in Sean's brain. Despite still being a little blurry, the driver looked familiar, but where the hell had he seen him before?

Turning to ask Brian a question, Sean smacked his shoulder again and grunted in agony. *Fuck!* He needed a goddamn painkiller after that impact.

A lightbulb went off in his brain. "Holy shit!"

His head whipped back to the screen, and he willed it to become discernible as the cameraman continued to fiddle with it. He knew he'd seen the guy before. Just one more adjustment, and he'd be certain.

"What?" Brian asked, sticking his head in the van.

"Hang on." Sean stared as the pixels danced once more, and the driver's picture came into focus. "Son of a fucking bitch! Can you print that?"

The cameraman nodded as his fingers flew over the keyboard. "Yeah, sure thing."

The fifteen-second wait for the photo to print was excruciating, and Sean ripped it from the console's printer before the last few lines of pixels were added. Ignoring his throbbing shoulder, he jumped out of the van while everyone stared at him expectantly.

He looked at the sheriff. "Have a deputy get names and a phone number for these guys. They'll get their exclusive, but not before we get Grace back and nail this fucking bastard." He glared at the other newsman. "Follow us, and you get nothing, understand?"

"Yes, sir!"

Pivoting, he pulled open the back door to Grace's business. It was the fastest way to get to his car out front, and Tim was still there to lock up. Brian was on Sean's heels as Rafe and Lynch ran toward the latter's department vehicle to meet them on the street, clueless as to where they were going at the moment.

Brian followed his brother out the front door. "You going to tell me who the hell that is and where we're going?"

Sean yanked on his driver's door. "We're going to see a psycho pharmacist."

Grace woke up in a fog to sheer silence. Her mouth felt like she'd swallowed a pound of cotton, and her head throbbed. *What the hell did I drink last night to get a*

hangover like this? Heck, she couldn't even remember the last time she'd been hungover.

She tried to roll over and find her pillow at the same time, but something was wrong. Not only could she not find her pillow, but she also wasn't even in her bed.

Oh, shit! I'm not in a bed at all and can't move my arms or legs!

It took her a moment to realize her immobility came from her limbs being restrained, although that didn't make her feel any better. In fact, it was really, really bad. Blinking several times, she tried to bring the surrounding area into focus. She was in a room with no windows. A bare bulb hung above her, and around her, against the walls, were cabinets and shelves. It was a storage room of sorts, and she was lying on a table.

Grace yanked on her arms and legs, but she was securely fastened with leather straps attached to chains. The rattling sent chills down her spine.

Panicking, she opened her mouth. "Help! Somebody, help! Please! Help!"

Tears overflowed onto her cheeks, and she screamed her throat raw, but no one answered. The dryness in her mouth made her cough, and she tried to clear her throat.

How did I get here? Who brought me here, and where are they now? And where the fuck is "here"?

Wherever "here" was, she hoped Sean or the police would find her—and soon.

But how? Do they even know I'm missing?

Grace resumed her screaming and pulled at her restraints until her arms ached and her voice was hoarse. Her heaving chest hurt, and her face was now wet from a combination of tears and sweat. Her body sagged against the hard table.

"Please, Sean," she whispered into the ensuing silence. "Please be my hero and find me."

Barreling into the pharmacy, Sean ignored the startled look on the faces of the employees and customers. Brian, Lynch, and Rafe followed him. On the way there, after Brian had called the car behind them with their destination, the sheriff's detective had turned on his lights and sirens and then pulled in front of Sean's Mustang to lead the way. Either way, the federal agent would have broken every traffic law to get to the pharmacy. They made the ten-minute ride from Whisper to Nags Head, near the hospital, in five minutes flat.

Gripping the photo printout a little too tightly, Sean vaulted over the counter to the pharmacist's work area. The female pharmacist gasped in alarm, and another woman, probably a pharmacy tech, screamed, but her cry was cut short when Sean shoved the picture in her face. "Who the fuck is this?"

"Sean," Brian warned from the other side of the counter. "Easy." He smiled at the tech, who appeared to be in shock, and showed her his department ID. "Ma'am, I'm Special Agent Brian Malone of the State Bureau of Investigations. Can you tell us who the man in the photo is?"

The calm voice did nothing to stop the woman from shaking with fear. Her gaze slowly moved to Brian, Rafe, and Lynch before returning to the scary man in front of her.

Sean waved the picture in her face again, but bit back the words on the tip of his tongue. The pharmacist, who was less rattled at the sudden intrusion, stepped forward, put her hand on her coworker's arm, and gently pushed her out of the way so she could look at the photo. "That's George."

"George who?" Sean practically growled.

"Wallace. George Wallace. He's a pharmacist here." Her eyes went wide as she concluded that the reason why they were looking for her coworker wasn't good. "Why are you asking?"

"Where does he live, ma'am?" Brian asked.

"I-I don't know." She turned to the other woman. "Sherry, do you know?"

A very pale Sherry just squeaked and shook her head violently.

The pharmacist turned back to Sean. "His address is on file in the office." She pointed to the door behind him. "If you let me pass, I'll get it for you."

He gave her a curt nod and stepped aside, a little too close for comfort for Sherry, who flinched. Finally realizing he'd been scaring the shit out of her, he gave her a tense smile. "I'm sorry, but it's a matter of life and death."

Her only answer was an uncontrolled bobbing of her head. Pivoting, he followed the pharmacist into a small office, where she pulled open the top drawer of a filing cabinet and selected a folder toward the back. Pulling out the top page, she held it at an angle so she and Sean could both see the information. The others stood in a small hallway outside the open door because there was not enough room for all of them.

The woman pointed to an address located in Nags Head. "Six-one-zero Park Terrace, in the Forest Glen condominiums."

Sean was about to thank her when something caught his eye. Another address was above that one and had been crossed out. "Did he move recently?"

"Yes. Well, a few months ago. He moved here from Pennsylvania when his aunt died about six months ago. From what I understand, her house needs a lot of renovations before it's habitable, so he's living in the condo until it's done. He said he was doing the renovations himself. That's the address for the house, I believe."

Pushing past the others, Sean said, "Thirty-eight Pelican Lane, Manns Harbor. Brad, send units to the Forest Glen condos just in case, but my bet is on Manns Harbor."

He prayed he was right. Grace's life depended on it.

Chapter 22

George grumbled as he strode back up the driveway toward the detached garage. He'd been gone way longer than planned.

Fucking, whiny bitch.

First, it was the fucking lightbulb. Next came a dripping faucet. Then she'd asked him to put her Easter decorations up in the attic. He'd been *thisfuckingclose* to shoving her up there with all the dusty boxes and locking the trap door shut.

Finally, he'd offered to take her garbage to the curb on his way out, and she jumped at the chance not to have to bring it there herself. One of these days...

Oh, well. There were plenty of other things he could do this evening to rid Mrs. Pain-in-the-ass Pennington from his mind, and they all involved the slut currently waiting for him.

He entered the garage and engaged the door's

deadbolt. As he took the stairs two at a time, he sorted through his keys for the one to the next lock. When he opened the door, the bitch started screaming, "Help! Somebody! Help!"

Quickly slamming the door and locking it, he stormed over to her and slapped her across the face. "Shut up, slut!"

"Who—who are you? Why are you doing this?"

"I'm your worst fucking nightmare," he snarled. "And your last."

The fear on her face was making him hard, but there were things he had to take care of first. Stepping over to a cabinet, he found the jar of pennies right where it should be. Each one was dated 1993—the year he'd killed his worthless excuse for a mother and turned his life around for the better.

It had been fate when his next kill had propositioned him years later. Before he'd left the prostitute's dead body in the dirty motel room she'd brought him to, a lone penny on the floor had caught his eye. When he picked it up and saw the year on it was 1993, he knew it was a sign that this was his calling in life, and he placed it on her forehead. He'd been collecting them ever since, choosing the shiniest ones for his masterpieces.

"Please tell me why you're doing this. If you're going... going to k-kill me, I have a right to understand why."

Her voice was trembling but soft. She hadn't

shouted but had spoken as if she were speaking to a small child. Pivoting slowly, George stared at the slut. She was still scared but wanted to know—wanted to understand. None of the sluts before her had ever said that to him. Oh, they'd screamed, "Why are you doing this?" but never that they wanted to understand.

He'd known she would be different than the others —she wasn't a party girl. But she was still a slut. Maybe this one time, he would let his victim know why he was going to kill her and turn her into his next masterpiece.

* * *

Sean remembered his tactical training and parked a house away from the suspect's home. Lynch and a marked deputy's car pulled up behind him. The occupants poured out of the vehicles and met beside the Mustang just as Sean's cell phone rang. Glancing at the screen, he saw it was Matt Griffin and answered it. "What?"

"Judge Sellers says you have reasonable cause to search for Grace and nothing else. Don't open anything or look anywhere she can't be hidden. For everything else, you have to wait for an official search warrant, or it's inadmissible. Got it?"

Sean nodded even though the other man couldn't see him. "Yeah, got it."

"I'm about five minutes out, but don't wait for me."

Disconnecting the call, he addressed the others.

"Grace only. Everything else has to wait." He pointed at the two uniformed deputies. "Go around back, and don't let him know you're there. Check if anything is unlocked or if you can see in the windows, but don't enter without my okay."

The two men started up the neighbor's drive and would cut through the backyard.

"Want to play dumb and ring the doorbell or go in like gangbusters?" Rafe asked.

Sean was about to respond when a little voice sounded from behind him. "Excuse me."

Spinning around, he found a little old lady peering up at him with wide eyes. "Yes, ma'am?"

"I live over there." She pointed at the house directly across from Wallace's. "Is everything all right?"

This could work to their advantage. "Ma'am, I'm Special Agent Sean Malone from the FBI. Do you know your neighbor across the street, Mr. George Wallace?"

"Of course. Such a nice man. He was just visiting with me. He's always coming over to help me with the chores this old body can't do anymore." It was clear she thought the man was a saint. Her gaze bounced from lawman to lawman before going back to Sean. "Why do you ask?"

Sean ignored her question, fighting the urge to storm Wallace's house and rescue Grace. They needed all the intelligence they could get to ensure the bastard didn't escalate and kill her swiftly. The man liked to toy with his victims, and if he'd been over at this woman's house, that meant he'd had very little time with Grace so far.

"You say he was just over at your house? When did he get there, and how long ago did he leave?"

"Why, he was helping me for about half an hour and left just a few minutes ago. He took out my trash and then went into his garage. I think he has a workshop or something on the second floor, since whenever he's here, he's either renovating the house or he's in the garage."

Thank God for nosy neighbors!

"Not sure why he's renovating though," she added, "because Susan, his aunt—God rest her soul—kept the house updated and clean. And she had it decorated so beautifully and—"

Rafe stepped forward, interrupting the woman. "You're sure he's still in the garage, ma'am?"

"Yes. He only went in there a few minutes before you got here. As a matter of fact, I'm baking him a Bundt cake right now to thank him for all he does for me."

If Sean had his way, Wallace wouldn't be getting the Bundt cake—he'd be eating shit in prison or burning in Hell. "Thanks for your help, ma'am. Why don't you head back inside? You don't want that cake to get overcooked."

Her eyes widened. "Oh, you're right. There's nothing worse than the smell of burnt food. Now, don't tell George I'm making it for him—I don't want to spoil the surprise."

"Our lips are sealed, ma'am."

Any hope they had of her returning to her house immediately was lost when she asked, "Why did you say you were looking for George again? He's such a nice man. If you want, I could introduce you to him and—"

While she'd been rambling, another uniformed deputy arrived on the scene, and Sean waved him over before interrupting the older woman. He spoke loud enough for the approaching man to hear him. "Ma'am, this deputy will need your contact information and has some more questions for you. He can do that inside your home so you can check on that cake, all right?"

"Oh..." She eyed the deputy and then faced Sean again. "Of course, yes. Are you sure you don't need me to introduce—"

"No, ma'am, we've got it covered. Thank you." Sean gave his head a subtle tilt toward her residence. "Deputy, if you could take care of that, I'd appreciate it."

The man coughed what sounded like "bullshit" into his fist and then pasted on a fake grin. "Sure, no problem."

As the woman was escorted away, the men started for Wallace's property. They met the other uniformed deputies at the top of the driveway, and before the two could report anything, Sean signaled that their target was in the garage. He gestured for them to head around the back of the small building in case of a rear exit or windows.

Brian quietly stepped over to the pedestrian door on the side of the building. The overhead doors were a last resort, as lifting them would alert Wallace.

Finding the door locked, Sean's brother pulled the small lock pick set from the inside pocket of his jacket. Everyone else pulled their weapons from their holsters. Brian had the lock undone in under a minute, then put away the pick and drew his own gun. As quietly as he could, he turned the knob and opened the door. Rafe and Sean tactically rounded the door jamb like they'd been partnered for years. Weapons out in front of them, they scanned the garage's interior. The white car Wallace had been driving earlier was parked on the far side. Meanwhile, in the closest parking spot was a gray Toyota Camry with damage to the front passenger side, right where it'd made contact with Sean's body a few days ago.

Brian tapped Sean on the shoulder and pointed at a set of wooden stairs leading to the enclosed second-floor loft. A closed door called to them from the top of the stairs. Sean led the way, moving as fast as he dared without making a sound. When he reached the door, he tried the knob and found it locked. This time, he was foregoing the lock-pick route. Busting the door down would get them in a lot faster and hopefully shock Wallace to the point he'd freeze before he hurt Grace.

Taking a half step back, Sean shifted his weight onto his left leg and lifted his right foot.

Keep him talking, Grace. Give Sean a chance to figure out that you're missing and who has you. But how the hell is he going to figure out the serial killer is a mild-mannered pharmacist who wears a white coat at work? White is the color the good guys always wear, right? Just keep praying Sean puts it all together and rescues you in time! Keep the psycho talking. Fall back on your psychology training. It had been a required course—use it now! It's the only chance you have to give Sean more time!

It had taken a few minutes of the man's cruel face bouncing around her memory before she finally recognized him. She had no idea what his name was, but she was certain he was the pharmacist whom she'd handed Sean's prescription to a few days ago.

The man stared at her, hopefully mulling over her last question, so she repeated it. "Why are you doing this? Did I do something to make you mad? Did those other women? I'm sorry if I did. It was never my intention to insult or hurt you." *Try to get him to humanize you. See you as a good person, not as someone he wants to kill.* "My—my name is Grace, I'm a physical therapist. Did you know that?"

He tilted his head, and his eyes narrowed like he was uncertain. But still, he remained silent as he stared at her. Her eyes flitted to his hand, and her gut clenched as she saw him slowly twirling a knife between his fingers. It was a Leatherman knife, like the one her father owned, similar to a Swiss Army knife.

Trying not to panic, she swallowed hard, and her gaze returned to his. "I don't even know your name."

That seemed to catch him off guard. The confusion in his eyes deepened. "Why do you want to know my name?"

"I-I guess it's—it's a habit—when I tell someone my name, I like to know theirs."

"*Hmmm.* You're not like the others." He stepped forward, the knife still spinning between his fingers as if he didn't even realize he was doing it.

"I-I'm not?"

"No. The others didn't ask questions like you." Another step toward her.

Grace's arms ached from the position they were in and from the struggle earlier. Her chest hurt. Her heart was pounding so hard, she was shocked he didn't hear it. Her mouth was dry, and she was surprised she hadn't peed her pants from the fear coursing through her veins.

Taking a deep breath, she asked, "D-does it bother you that I'm asking questions?"

"George. My name is George."

"That's a nice name, George."

He snarled, and she flinched. "Nice name? Nice name! It's not a nice fucking name! It's a name that got me picked on in school! And did that bitch care she gave me a faggot name? No!"

Spittle shot from his lips as his face turned red.

"I-I'm s-sorry!"

As he took another step forward, the rage on his face told Grace he would kill her no matter what. She'd fucked up.

"You have no idea what sorry is! Sorry? That's a fucking laugh! Do you know what that slut did? How she sold herself for drugs while giving me spare change, telling me to go to the fucking movies while she fucked her johns? Then she'd be high as fuck when I got home and couldn't even feed me! Instead of buying her own son food with her sex money, she just blew it up her damn nose! That fucking cunt!"

His arm swung up, holding the knife high, and Grace screamed. This was it, she was going to die!

A loud bang startled both of them as the door splintered open. Yelled orders, Grace's shrieks, and George's roars were drowned out by the sound of gunfire. The man's body jolted as the bullets entered his chest, and bright, red blood shot out from his back in spurts, soaking his shirt and the wall behind him. He teetered on unsteady legs for a second or two before collapsing in a heap on the floor. His lifeless eyes stared up at Grace.

"Grace! Grace! It's me! Hush! You're all right! *Sh,* baby!"

She hadn't known she was still screaming until Sean's shouts finally reached her ears. Her body had also thrashed uncontrollably, but now, as her gaze met Sean's, her movements eased, but she still trembled.

Sean cupped her head in his hands, demanding she focus on him. "It's okay, baby. It's okay. I'm here."

Suddenly, her arms and legs were free, and she then noticed Brian, Rafe, and Brad Lynch in the room. She burst into tears as Sean helped her sit up. Placing an arm under her knees and another at her lower back, he lifted her in his arms. As she buried her face in his chest, he carried her out of the room.

It was over. She was safe. And she never wanted Sean to let her go again.

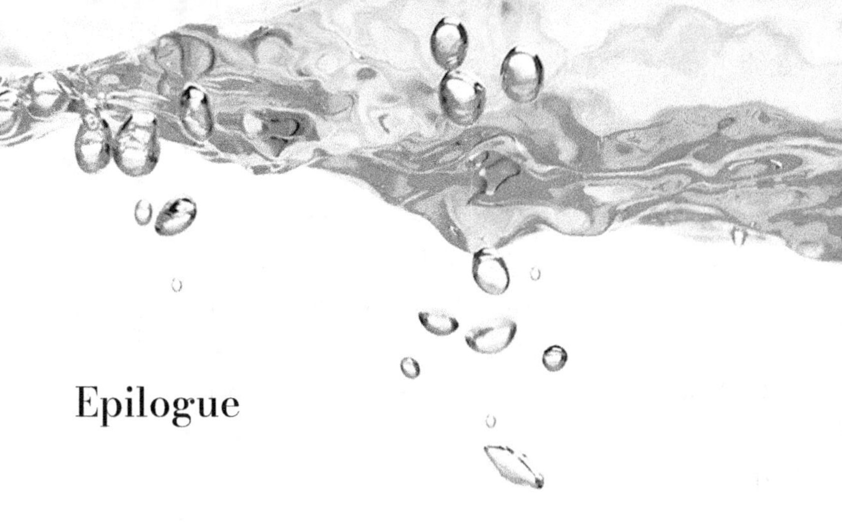

Epilogue

Sean held Grace's hand as they sat with Bonnie and Dan in the hospital's Labor and Delivery waiting room in Little Creek, Virginia. Moriah was going on her ninth hour of labor, and still no sign of the next generation of Malones. She'd woken KC up at 4:00 a.m., and after a mad dash to the hospital, he'd texted everyone. Their little convoy of vehicles had arrived just after 9:00, and four hours later, they were still waiting.

Sean's thumb caressed the back of Grace's hand as he watched the news. Three days after rescuing her from that bastard's clutches, his heart still hadn't begun beating normally yet, and he was constantly finding ways to touch her. He needed to reassure himself she was alive and unharmed. Her sleep had been interrupted multiple times by nightmares, and every night he held her close, doing his best to banish them from her mind.

Through Grace's recount of what Wallace had said to her, the evidence they'd found in his lair, and the man's background they'd been slowly piecing together, the making of a serial killer was coming to light. The Philadelphia Police Department and Special Agent Karen Winslow had investigated Wallace's history in their area.

The man had been born and raised in a poor area of the city. His mother had been a junkie who'd been in and out of jail, while he'd been placed in temporary foster homes. It appeared the system had failed him because he was repeatedly returned to his mother's care even though it was clear she'd neglected him.

According to the PPD, Lisa Wallace had been murdered in 1993, when her son was fifteen. It had been an unsolved case all these years, with the assumption one of her johns or drug connections had done the dirty deed.

But now, it seemed George had murdered his mother. She'd been strangled with a scarf, the same way he'd killed his other victims, and loose change—dimes, nickels, quarters, and pennies—had been scattered around her body. From Grace's interview, they'd learned the significance of the coins. For some unknown reason, the killer had focused on the pennies, and Dr. Suki Ralston believed it was because the penny was worth the least.

Suki also believed that the reason Wallace had waited so long between his kills in Pennsylvania and North Carolina was that he'd hoped his newfound windfall would make up for the life he'd grown up in. But the murders had already become an irrational way to get back at his mother, and it had just been a matter of time before the craving to find a new victim was too potent to ignore.

His aunt's lawyer had come forward after hearing what had happened on the news and explained that Susan Wallace had left instructions in her will for her nephew to be found. They would never know why she'd waited until after her death to have him contacted.

Sean glanced over at Bonnie and Dan. Like Grace and him, they were holding hands, and Sean grinned. It made him happy the two had finally realized there was more to their relationship than just friendship. He wouldn't be surprised if they beat Grace and him to the altar.

Yeah, he was definitely going to ask her to marry him someday, but first, he wanted her to recover from this ordeal. Matt Griffin had given Sean the name of the psychologist his department used for any of the deputies who experienced a horrific call or were involved in a shooting. The female doctor was pleasant, and Grace felt comfortable speaking with her yesterday. She was scheduled for one-hour sessions, three times a week, for the next month.

In the meantime, Tim was doing his best to hold down the fort at Grace's business while she dealt with the aftermath of being kidnapped by a serial killer. With her approval, he'd asked another therapist he'd known for a long time to fill in for the next week. If the woman worked out, Grace was going to hire her part-time.

Sean's boss had told him to take the rest of his vacation time if he wanted to after the case was officially closed. He'd decided to take the offer so he could spend as much time with Grace as possible, getting her through the nightmares and everything else.

Footsteps in the hallway had him looking up, and Brian came in with several bags from a nearby deli. He was just about to start handing out the sandwiches when KC stuck his head around the doorjamb. "Anyone want to meet little Megan Malone?"

"Yes!" Bonnie and Grace squealed at the same time.

Everyone stood as the new dad stepped into the room, holding his daughter, wrapped in a pink blanket and wearing a matching pink cap. KC cradled her like an expert. "I can only keep her out here for a minute. She came out healthy and screaming at the top of her lungs."

"She's beautiful, KC," Bonnie gushed.

"Adorable," Grace agreed.

KC looked at Uncle Dan with a warm smile. "We'd like you to be her godfather."

Tears filled the older man's eyes, and he swallowed hard. "I'd be honored, son."

"Bonnie, that means you're going to be her godmother," the new father announced.

The woman squealed again, which had little Megan twitching before she let out a yawn that seemed too big for such a little baby. "Oh, I'd love to, KC!"

Sean clapped his eldest brother on the back as he stared at the baby's little button nose. "You did good, brother. You and Moriah did really good. Congratulations."

* * *

Later that night, Dan and Bonnie held hands as they walked along the beach. It'd been a wonderful day, and once again all was right in their little part of the world. As they strolled, Jinx investigated every crab, clump of seaweed, and clamshell he could find.

Lifting his gaze to the sky, Dan stopped short. "Look. A shooting star."

Beside him, Bonnie sighed. "It must be Annie saying hello. Do you want to tell her or do you want me to?"

Dan chuckled. When KC and Moriah had fallen in love, he'd come to the beach one night to let his beloved Annie know she was doing a good job of watching over their nephews. "I told her last time. You can tell her this time."

Bonnie looked to the heavens. "Another one of the boys is in love, Annie. Now we just have to find Brian's happily-ever-after."

* * *

Coming soon! *Her Savior: Malone Brothers Book 3*

Want to know what's coming next? Join my Facebook Group - Samantha Cole's Sexy Six-Pack's Sirens...

Or sign up for my newsletter - samanthacolebooks.com/mailing-list

If you enjoyed *Her Sleuth*, check out *Cold Feet: Largo Ridge Book 1*, now available.

Some homecomings heal old wounds. Others open new possibilities...

Regina calls off her wedding at the last minute—she can't marry a man she loves but isn't in love with. Only one man falls into that category—Buck. However, after their one and only kiss years ago, he turned tail and ran, leaving her confused and heartbroken.

The last thing Buck expects, a few days after retiring from the military, is to inherit a ski resort. That solves his problem of trying to decide what to do now that he's a civilian again. But he also has to face his PTSD and one big regret head-on.

For six years, his best friend's sister, Regina, had been out of sight but not quite out of Buck's mind. Now, with them both living in Largo Ridge again, it's getting harder to ignore the attraction growing stronger between them.

Does Buck have the courage to stand up and love the woman his heart knows is his? And will Regina let him?

Other Books by Samantha Cole

*******Denotes titles/series that are only available on select digital sites. Paperbacks and audiobooks are available on most book sites.

THE TRIDENT SECURITY SERIES

Leather & Lace

His Angel

Waiting For Him

Not Negotiable

Topping The Alpha (MM)

Watching From the Shadows

Whiskey Tribute

Tickle His Fancy

No Way in Hell: A Steel Corp/Trident Security Crossover (co-authored with J.B. Havens)

Absolving His Sins

Option Number Three (MMF)

Salvaging His Soul

Trident Security Field Manual

Torn In Half

Burning For Him

***Heels, Rhymes, & Nursery Crimes Series
(with 13 other authors)
Jack Be Nimble: A Trident Security-Related Short Story

***The Deimos Series
Handling Haven: Special Forces: Operation Alpha
Cheating the Devil: Special Forces: Operation Alpha

The Trident Security Omega Team Series
Mountain of Evil
A Dead Man's Pulse
Forty Days & One Knight

The Doms of The Covenant Series
Double Down & Dirty (MFM)
Entertaining Distraction
Knot a Chance
Finding His Forever (MM)
Reclaiming His Soulmate

The Blackhawk Security Series
Tuff Enough
Blood Bound

Master Key Series
Master Key Resort

Scattered Moments in Time: A Collection of Short Stories &
More

Sweet Revenge

The Sugarplum Fairy (M/M)

*****THE BID ON LOVE SERIES**

(WITH 7 OTHER AUTHORS!)

Going, Going, Gone: Book 2

*****THE COLLECTIVE: SEASON TWO**

(WITH 7 OTHER AUTHORS!)

Angst: Book 7 (M/M)

SPECIAL COLLECTIONS

Trident Security Series: Volume I

Trident Security Series: Volume II

Trident Security Series: Volume III

Trident Security Series: Volume IV

Trident Security Series: Volume V

Trident Security Series: Volume VI

About Samantha Cole

USA Today Bestselling Author Samantha Cole is a retired police officer and paramedic who now writes heart-pounding romance in multiple forms—MF, MM, and ménage. From military heroes to rugged cowboys and small-town heat, her stories blend passion, loyalty, and danger in perfect balance.

Awards:

Wannabe in Wyoming (co-authored by J.B. Havens) won the bronze medal in the 2021 Readers' Favorite Awards in the General Romance category.

Scattered Moments in Time won the gold medal in the 2020 Readers' Favorite Awards in the Fiction Anthology category.

Where the Broken Bloom (formerly *The Road to Solace*) won the silver medal in the 2017 Readers' Favorite Awards in the Contemporary Romance category.

Sexy Six-Pack's Sirens Group on Facebook
Website: www.samanthacolebooks.com
Newsletter: samanthacolebooks.com/mailing-list

facebook.com/SamanthaColeAuthor

instagram.com/samanthacoleauthor

bookbub.com/profile/samantha-a-cole

goodreads.com/SamanthaCole

amazon.com/Samantha-A-Cole/e/B00X53K3X8

tiktok.com/@samanthacoleauthor

youtube.com/@SamanthaACole-bp6yu